WHAT IF... VOL. 1

Science Fiction and Paranormal Short Stories

TIM TROTT

TIM TROTT

I dedicate this book to my wife, Mari Trott, the best life decision I ever made.

I am also dedicating this book to the Daytona Writers Group and Veronica H. Hart. I had not written fiction, but Ronnie and the group urged me to try. Now I love writing fiction! My advice to any aspiring author is to find a local writer's group or join an online group on Reddit or Facebook. It's amazing how much a group of like-minded people can challenge, benefit, and teach you while expanding your writing skills and enjoyment.

If you enjoy this book, please take a few moments to write a nice review where you purchased it and recommend it to your friends and social media followers!

CONTENTS

Introduction	VI
How an Alien Saved the World	1
A Parallel Universe	14
The Time the Aliens Came	35
The Camera That Saw Through Time	43
We Saw the Aliens	51
If Dreams Could Speak	60
The Company Hired a Robot	73
Interview with an Alien	90
If Ghosts Could Talk	105
Date Night	115
About the Author	120

Introduction

I have my own take on science fiction. I often like to blur the lines between science fiction and non-fiction by weaving in some real-life facts. I don't crawl down rabbit holes, but I often harvest and recycle them. On the other hand, you might read something you think is fiction but isn't. One thing that is different about my science fiction writing is that I make reference to real science and sometimes include footnotes.

There's a quote I like from a very old poem by Mary T. Lathrap, *Walk a Mile in His Moccasins*:

"By walking in the shoes of a fictional character, by seeing through the eyes of the characters, the reader gains a different perspective. If we're lucky, that perspective teaches us a lesson in real life."

How an Alien Saved the World

T he story has continued for thousands of years, but this is as good a place as any to begin:

Japan Airlines (JAL) Flight 1628 – November 17th, 1986
- Location: Alien Patrol Sector *Mem* (Somewhere over Eastern Alaska)

- Altitude: 37,000 feet

- Ground Speed: 600 mph.

- Origin: Paris, France

- Destination: Tokyo, Japan, via Anchorage, Alaska.

- Cargo: Beaujolais wine.

As the Japan Airlines cargo jet passed over eastern Alaska, Captain Kenju Terauchi scanned the sky from the left seat in the cockpit. He looked about 2,000 feet below and saw two bright lights moving at the same speed as the jetliner. He turned to his co-pilot and first officer, Takanore Mori, and said, pointing below, "Do you see that?"

The co-pilot leaned forward and strained to see through the window. "What are they?"

"I don't know," the captain replied. He glanced over his right shoulder at Flight Engineer Yoshio Tsukuba. Tsukuba grimaced as he shook his head.

The two unknown objects swooped up in front of the jetliner, one above the other, keeping pace a short distance ahead, in an odd rocking motion. The strange craft appeared to have multiple rocket thrusters arranged in two rectangular rows, firing in sequence to perform the maneuver.

Pressing the radio button on the yoke, the captain called, "Anchorage Center, Japan Air sixteen twenty-eight, ah, do you have any traffic ah, in our path?"

Air Traffic Control responded[1] , "Japan Air 1628 heavy, negative."

The captain continued, "Japan Air sixteen twenty-eight, Roger. We have in sight two traffic in front of us, one mile about".

At that same moment, aboard one of the two alien ships, the pilot, Zork, communicated with the other alien ship with the equivalent of "Watch this!" The alien craft shifted to a side-by-side formation, still maintaining the same distance ahead of the Japan Airlines jet. The two rows of what appeared to be rocket thrusters arranged in a rectangle at the back of a more familiar saucer configuration made these particular spaceships unusual. The pilot

---

1. https://en.wikipedia.org/wiki/Japan_Air_Lines_Cargo_Flight_1628_incident - ATC recording

of the second ship, Zylox, expressed concern as he replied (in his language), "I'm not sure we should do this. If the Galaxy Council gets word, they could sanction us for breaking the Greada Treaty."

Both knew that, under the treaty, zooming airline pilots was not allowed. Realizing he might have made a mistake, Zork agreed. The two alien pilots engaged their nuclear ion antigravity propulsion and accelerated away at extreme velocity.

By the time Air Traffic Control vectored nearby United Airlines flight 69 to the area, the alien craft had vanished.

***

The Greada Treaty–1952

In 1952, the Gray aliens contacted certain US government agents. The government exhibited obvious reluctance to permit aliens to conduct operations in the country. To make their side of the argument, the Grays staged flights over the capital in Washington, D.C[2]. The activity received mostly little attention and did not cause the scandal that had been feared.

Coincidentally (or not), Project Bluebook took shape in March 1952, less than two weeks later. A flurry of UFO sightings in July of that year, especially in Washington, D.C., put Project Bluebook to the test. The aliens wanted to make a point. Seven or more alien craft appeared on the radar at Washington National Airport (later named after President Ronald Reagan). Another event involved a Navy warship.

These events did not escape the attention of the newly elected President Dwight Eisenhower. In the beginning, Ike rejected a face-to-face meeting with the aliens, but the aliens apparently gave assurances of peaceful intentions. Thus, on February 20th,

---

2. https://en.wikipedia.org/wiki/1952_Washington,_D.C.,_UFO_i
    ncident

1954, shortly after taking office, Ike quickly arranged for a mini vacation to California. It was unusual in that he had recently concluded a golf vacation in Georgia. However, the new president had more than golf on his schedule for this vacation.

Peter Carlson wrote about *Ike and the Aliens* later in the Washington Post[3] . As the Post described in the article, during President Eisenhower's vacation in Palm Springs, California, he briefly vanished. His staff used the excuse that the President had a loose crown and needed to make a quick trip to see a dentist. For a short time, the Associated Press reported Ike had died but quickly retracted the story. In reality, Ike had boarded a flight to nearby Edwards Airforce Base. The Air Force shut down the airbase for three hours. A small group of Nordic-looking aliens had landed at the base earlier in the day. The reason these particular aliens may have been selected is because they resembled humans, unlike the more commonly seen almond-eye Grays.

Air Force One, the Lockheed Constellation known as "Connie," was parked on the runway next to a large alien ship. Secret Service and base personnel were extremely uneasy about the new president going aboard the spacecraft alone to meet with the aliens. Discussion with the aliens was said to have centered on the scheduled hydrogen bomb test, known as Bravo, to be conducted at the Bikini Atoll. The meeting lasted almost 45 minutes and did not go well. After the meeting, Ike emerged from the alien spacecraft, hastening to his plane without speaking to anyone.

That would not be the last time there would be such a meeting.

After that first meeting, President Eisenhower established a permanent committee to monitor and conduct covert activities with the aliens under a treaty. The Greada Treaty was not finalized until a year later, when President Eisenhower again met with alien

---

3. https://www.washingtonpost.com/archive/lifestyle/2004/02/
   19/ike-and-the-alien-ambassadors/4698e544-1dc8-4573-8b
   8d-2b48d2a6305e/

representatives, this time at Holloman Airforce Base, in Hanger 17.
.

Treaties and agreements may have also been made between the aliens and the governments of Britain, Russia, and China at the same time.

Steven Spielberg used reports of that meeting as the basis for the movie Close Encounters of the Third Kind. In a scene in the movie, the character playing the part of French scientist Claude Lacombe talks about past UFO encounters with American military personnel, known as the "Eisenhower Close Encounters."

What follows has been drawn from common speculation:

The government finally conducted the Greada Treaty signing in secret, conveniently bypassing the Constitutionally required Senate ratification. President Eisenhower, possibly because of his military background, stood as the sole US President, aware of the agreement with alien forces. The document remains classified *Above Top Secret*. Even President Jimmy Carter[4] , who had openly acknowledged his own personal UFO experience, was not granted access to the information.

The terms of the treaty were said to have promised aliens would not interfere in our government's affairs, and the government would not interfere in theirs. The US Government would keep the aliens' presence on our planet secret. In exchange, the government would share in a limited amount of alien advanced technology. It was also understood in the agreement that the government would overlook the abduction of humans and animals for medical examination and study. The aliens agreed to return humans who had been subjected to abduction to the place of the abduction, with no memory of what had happened. Under the treaty, the aliens were to maintain their own secret facilities on our planet. Part of the agreement also involved the exchange of ambassadors.

A variety of alien lifeforms took part in the final agreement, including Grays, which ranged from tall aliens standing 9 feet tall to a smaller variety less than three feet in height. Also, rumors

---

4. https://en.wikipedia.org/wiki/Jimmy_Carter_UFO_incident

suggest that the agreement included the Andromedans, Annukaki, and possibly the human-like Nordics or Pleiadians, who had been involved in the initial meeting. There were indications the subterranean Earth Reptilians wanted no part in the arrangement.

Many years later, the granddaughter of Dwight David Eisenhower appeared in an interview[5] that can be found on YouTube[6].

The interviewer began by saying, "I've heard a lot about some rumors that I'm hoping you can either confirm or deny for me. I'm going to come right out and ask you: Do you believe that your great grandfather, Dwight D. Eisenhower, signed a treaty with extra-terrestrials?"

Laura Eisenhower answered, "It's a true story. What I've learned about Eisenhower's relationship to extraterrestrial beings and ET-government treaties is that supposedly, in 1954, there was a meeting at Edwards Air Force Base."

"Right," the interviewer acknowledged as Laura Eisenhower continued.

"They seemed to have diplomatic intentions. The treaty had to do with bartering exchanges of planetary goods, natural resources, and compounds, and it was in exchange for [allowing} things like abductions."

The interviewer asked, "Why would they want to abduct humans? What are they doing with that?"

Laura responded, "They need our DNA. We have a treasure of DNA that is basically a living library." She explained that the aliens need to explore human DNA in their quest to unlock secrets of the Universe, which hide in the DNA of all living creatures.

The interviewer posed the question, why is it that every nuclear facility worldwide has been under extraterrestrial surveillance?

---

5. The clip is from an interview with Project Camelot, which propagates various conspiracy theories without evidence. This context diminishes the credibility.

6. https://www.youtube.com/watch?v=-FHaGFkHULo 2:06

Dr. Steven Greer[7] has provided a plausible explanation: "There is a scaler pulse coincident with a nuclear explosion that travels at multiples of the speed of light. That pulse is in the entangled aspect of quantum physics, and it disrupts extraterrestrial travel and communications."

***

Malmstrom Air Force Base, Montana – March 24th, 1967

A few minutes after sunset, a large, cigar-shaped space vehicle hovered high above the sprawling 13,800-acre Malmstrom Air Force Base in Montana. On that base, the Air Force 341st Missile Wing had responsibility for the operation and maintenance of a complex of ten Minuteman III intercontinental ballistic missiles, or ICBMs. The aliens aboard the specially equipped spaceship had a new device to try out. They had developed the device from data gathered from various missile complexes, specifically at Vandenberg Air Force Base in California and Minot Air Force Base in North Dakota. They were ready to test an Ion-Disruptor device.

It is said the device could generate a focused field of disruptive ionic resonance which interfered with electromagnetic systems within its range. In operation, the emitter mounted on the base of the alien ship projected a pulsating red glow to the ground below. They had used a smaller version of the device against a Navy fighter intent on shooting down an alien craft over the Gulf of Mexico. The disruptor successfully froze the fighter's offensive weapon controls, shielding the alien ship from attack. As the plane left the area, the Navy plane's electronics returned to normal.

This time, the test was larger. Tests would take place at other installations, including Plesetsk Cosmodrome and Baikonur Cosmodrome in Russia, Dongfeng Missile Base in China, India's missile test facilities, and Sainshand Missile Test Site in Mongolia, among

---

7. https://www.youtube.com/watch?v=45x5cWEdy9Q

others. The goal involved testing the disruptor's capability to disable multiple missile launch systems to stop nuclear war.

As the alien device activated, a bright red glow filled the sky.

A red warning light flashed in the underground control room. Sergeant Thomas, a security guard on duty, muttered, "What the hell is going on?"

Private Ramirez was also on duty that day. "Could it be a malfunction?"

The sergeant's training had taught him not to take chances. He contacted the base commander.

"Colonel Johnson, sir, we've got a situation here. The warning lights are acting up."

The colonel asked, "How many of our assets are affected, sergeant?"

Thomas scanned the control panels. All the control panels displayed anomalies, and the missile status indicators wavered between operational and offline. "It began with one, but now I'm seeing offline errors on all ten silos," Thomas reported.

"I need to notify Washington and call NORAD. I'll secure the base and get the technicians down there to find the problem. Let me know immediately if there is any change."

Before the colonel could end the call, the red lights stopped blinking, and all the consoles went back to normal.

"Wait," the sergeant said. "Whatever it was, the problem cleared up."

"I'm still sending technicians to find out what is going on down there."

As the colonel leaned back in his chair, he took a deep breath. His phone rang. It was the MP guard at the front gate.

"Colonel, this is Corporal Mitchel. I didn't want to bother you, but I thought I should let you know about something."

"Go on," the colonel replied, with a mix of concern and curiosity.

"Well," the corporal continued, "We saw this light—a bright red light. It was coming from this, well, this thing that was hovering over the base. It started pulsating for a little while, and about the time I was going to notify you, it stopped. It shot straight up out of sight. It's gone now, but I thought you should know."

What the MP saw was the alien ship with the device that had proven successful at disabling all ten launch systems.

The colonel thanked the corporal and assured him he had done the right thing. He considered including that detail in his report on the incident, but he decided not to pursue the matter further.

Why do people in the military resist talking about UFO encounters? In 1948, the U.S. government published document number 146, known as JANAP. The acronym stands for Joint Army Navy Air Publication. It criminalized public disclosure of information about UFO sightings, subjecting offenders to prosecution under the Espionage Act. The penalties included fines of $10,000 and up to ten years in prison. JANAP 146 later underwent declassification and was replaced by Air Force Manual (AFMAN) 10-206 in 1997. That new manual addressed the procedures for reporting and recording UFO sightings, but contained no explicit restrictions on discussing UFO-related information. However, those who report such incidents could be subject to a Non-Disclosure Agreement.

***

Maui, Hawaii–January 13th, 2018

As the sun rose over the Hawaiian landscape, locals and tourists enjoyed the tropical paradise. In a small office in the Hawaii Emergency Management Agency, David Mitchell sat at his desk, monitoring the state's emergency alert system. He was responsible for ensuring the smooth operation of the system, including sending important notifications in times of crisis. Meanwhile, Sarah Bennett, his co-worker, focused on her own tasks, occasionally glancing at monitors displaying the various emergency channels.

The calm of the morning abruptly broke when an urgent message popped up on David's computer screen. He read the alert in disbelief.

"BALLISTIC MISSILE THREAT INBOUND TO HAWAII. SEEK IMMEDI-ATE SHELTER. THIS IS NOT A DRILL."

David struggled to comprehend the situation as he turned to Sarah. "Sarah, look at this! We have a ballistic missile threat to Hawaii!" His tone was a mixture of panic and disbelief.

Sarah's eyes widened, and she gasped as she read the message and realized the magnitude of the situation.

In a flurry of well-rehearsed activity, David and Sarah sprang into action, alerting their superiors who initiated the emergency protocol. As panic spread across the island, sirens wailed, and residents scrambled to find shelter. David's fingers trembled as he typed on his keyboard. The message flashed across the screens of the television monitors mounted on the office walls. Radio stations were spreading the message to their audiences. A push alert appeared on cell phones on all the islands.

Meanwhile, a group of friends were enjoying the weather on a boat when they heard the alert on the marine radio. As they got closer to shore, they could see people running and screaming in the streets.

After 38 minutes, a new message appeared on David's screen:

"FALSE ALARM. THERE IS NO MISSILE THREAT TO HAWAII. FALSE ALARM."

David and Sarah stared at each other. The gravity of the false alarm weighed heavily on them. As they and the island residents regained their composure, the false alarm served as a stark re-minder of the threats that could strike at any moment, even in the most idyllic of settings.

As the new message spread, people began coming out of hiding, trying to make sense of what had happened.

***

SSBN 888 Prometheus – earlier that day.

Far out at sea, between Hawaii and the Republic of Kiribati, Commander James Anderson stood at the helm of the nuclear missile submarine, USS Prometheus. Through the periscope, he gazed at the expanse of the Pacific Ocean glistening in the morning sun. The submarine bobbed on the surface, its engines humming below decks.

A young officer, Lieutenant Ethan Roberts, broke the morning calm as he burst into the room.

"Commander, I have an urgent message. There's a missile inbound for Hawaii. Fleet Command in Pearl Harbor has issued the order to launch a response."

The Commander's brows furrowed as he took the message from the young officer's hand and scanned it carefully, his mind racing with doubts and uncertainty. He knew what this meant, the dire consequences that a wrong move could bring, not only for his crew, but on the world at large.

Shaking the paper in his hand at the other officer, he voiced his skepticism. "Are you certain about this, Lieutenant? We can't afford to make a hasty decision. Verify the authenticity of this order immediately," he commanded.

The lieutenant nodded, his face showing mounting anxiety, as he hurriedly stepped back into the communications station in the next compartment and began the confirmation process with Third Fleet Command in Pearl Harbor.

Meanwhile, Commander Anderson waited as tension escalated in the command center. The weight of the decision pressed heavily on the commander's shoulders, and doubts tugged at his mind, along with a nagging feeling that something wasn't right.

Lieutenant Roberts returned. He had confirmed the order from US3FLEET. Commander Anderson nodded toward the Lieutenant as he reminded everyone in the room, "We have a mission to accomplish. Proceed with the launch sequence."

Two officers, Strategic Weapons Officer Lieutenant David Ramirez and Lieutenant Commander Julia Stephens, stood side by side, their fingers hovering over the buttons that would unleash the deadly missile on the target in North Korea. They exchanged a glance, their expressions reflecting a mixture of fear and obedience. They both gulped in a breath of air as they pushed the buttons simultaneously, their actions laden with a heavy sense of responsibility. And then...

Nothing happened.

A short time later, to the relief of everyone aboard the submarine, the Stand-Down order arrived from Hawaii Fleet Command.

High above the submarine hovered an Aleph-type alien spaceship, a newer model of the one that crashed near Roswell. Aboard the alien ship were Zork and Commander Xelrok, assigned to patrol the Zayin Sector. As the sensors detected the submarine arming the missile system, Zork, and Xelrok activated an alien Ion Disruptor device that halted the submarine's launch system until the danger cleared. The task completed, Zork set the Interdimensional Gravitational Engine for the secret alien base. The craft first angled to one side and disappeared.

And that's how a space alien saved the world.

***

Fact or Fiction?

In a summary of this story, I asked the question *fiction or science?* Another question might be, how many science fiction stories include footnotes?

JAL Flight 1628 occurred on November 17th, 1986. The cockpit conversation is fictional, but the crew names are real. We transcribed the communications between the pilot and Air Traffic Control from the Air Traffic Control recording. United Flight 19 was also involved. The crew later related a description of the alien craft and their actions.

Multiple "sources" contributed information about the Greada Treaty. A detailed description of the purported event can be found (pp. 72 and 286) in the book Galactic Diplomacy by Michael E.

Salla, Ph.D[8] The author derived the details of those events from the testimonies of participants included in that book. The 2022 YouTube video provided the source for transcribing the quotations from the interview with Eisenhower's granddaughter. (Footnote link provided at the end of this chapter).

The JANAP and AFMAN government documents are real, and they include descriptions of UFO reporting.

The dialog in the story of the ICMB base at Malmstrom Air Force Base in Montana is total fiction. The description of the alien craft with the red beam, however, is based on reports that were filed on March 24th, 1967. In the story, Colonel Johnson is a fictionalized version of Captain Robert Salas, who was the commander of the 341st Missile Wing when the event is said to have occurred.

Hawaii's false alarm on January 13th, 2018, was widely reported by several news networks, including CNN[9].

The submarine incident is entirely fictional, as you may have guessed. However, the fact that the Navy Third Fleet is in Hawaii suggests the possibility that such an event could have occurred, given the circumstances.

Which brings us back to the question: is this story fiction or science? It is a blend of the two, with generous liberties taken with the timeline. As to the truth or fiction of the underlying theme of aliens and nuclear weapons ... that is for the reader to consider:

What if?

---

8. https://www.amazon.com/Galactic-Diplomacy-Dr-Michael-Salla/dp/0982290217

9. https://www.cnn.com/2018/01/13/politics/hawaii-missile-threat-false-alarm/index.html

A Parallel Universe

2 9 May, 2020

"There it goes," somebody in the office building at Kennedy Space Center shouted. The low rumbling in the distance grew louder, shaking the building. James Cooper glanced out from the window behind his chair. In the time it took for the sound to travel the two miles from Launch Complex 4, the contrails from the Chinese rocket already stretched into the clouds.

George was one of the 200-some people on the launch crew, working in close quarters on consoles. Because of COVID-19, they wore the face masks required by the CDC guidelines.

James and George became friends while working on the shuttle program. George, ten years James' senior, had thinning hair with traces of gray. Both men bore the distinguish markings of being married and well-fed, but not what you would call heavy. James, the taller of the two, still had most of the thick brown hair of his youth.

Rocket scientists, like James, get to go home at a regular time most days, but George and the rest of the launch crew had to be there to push the buttons at any hour. George was part of the launch crew for SpaceX that Saturday afternoon. His role in the launch crew was communication and tracking for the Falcon 9. Crew Dragon, with Endeavor Astronauts Bob Behnken and Doug Hurley on board. They would make history as the first crewed mission for SpaceX and Falcon 9, putting an end to NASA's dependence on Russia for transporting crews to the ISS.

Working at KSC since the 1980s, George had a few stories he liked to tell, especially about UFOs. His job involved monitoring communications; some of what he had heard had raised his curiosity. George had become convinced that astronauts had seen signs of extraterrestrials more than once.

It happened during Apollo 8. Module commander Walter Schirra said, "Please inform that there is a Santa Claus." Had they seen something unusual? Was it a code word? As the Apollo 11 crew later orbited the moon, a crew member also mentioned something on the "dark" side. But CAPCOM (Capsule Communicator) in Houston quickly interrupted, instructing the crew to "Switch to kilo." Kilo is a classified radio channel and not something NASA management would discuss publicly.

As expected, by 05:30, the post-launch traffic had largely cleared. Leaving the building, James squinted against the bright afternoon sun. Despite sunset being after 8 pm this time of year, the sun would be in his eyes all the way home to Orlando on Highway 50. He had not considered that fact before choosing a home east of his job. George wasn't a rocket scientist, at least not a physicist, but he was smart enough to live nearby in Titusville. That meant a direct route and a much shorter drive south from the space complex, avoiding the direct sun. The downside was when called to duty at KSC, George could get there on short notice.

The Cooper home, east of Orlando had been constructed in the mid-1980s. It had a small lawn and a two-car garage featuring his and hers Hondas. The design featured white siding with brick accents at the doorway. As James arrived, Judy was sorting through the mailbox at the curb. The drive from her job in nearby Longwood meant she got home early. James and Judy were about the same age, now in their mid-40s. Judy had changed little from when they had met at Titusville High, at least that was how James saw her. She had been his high school sweetheart. Her hair retained a natural light brown, in a style that complemented her face.

Judy's parents had moved from her birthplace in Chicago to Titusville, seeking refuge from the harsh Chicago weather. Her father had a management position at a local food chain. Following in her father's footsteps, Judy had pursued an MBA at nearby Stetson University in Deland.

In contrast, James' father worked as a science and math teacher. Driven by his desire to be a part of the space program, James chose the University of Central Florida in Orlando (then FTU), where he earned a Master of Science degree in physics and Planetary Science.

The couple continued to date throughout their college years and married soon after graduation. James graduated with a physics degree, and although they faced challenges in the initial years, they could eventually buy a comfortable home. They deliberately avoided having children, focusing instead on their careers, paying off college loans, and mortgages.

Around the time of the STS-63 launch, with the first female shuttle pilot, Eileen Collins, Judy assumed her position as manager for a local department store. James joined a NASA contractor team.

The STS-53 mission marked the first phase of the International Space Station Program and involved a rendezvous with the Russian Mir space station. James' initial assignment was to handle the complex calculations for this rendezvous, which presented a formidable challenge from the outset.

The history of NASA was uneven. The Space Shuttle disaster led President George W. Bush to terminate the program in 2011. That decision resulted in NASA being left to rely on Russia for Space Station supplies for over the course of nine years. As a result, many at the launch complex lost their jobs. While some individuals found work in the nearby defense industry in Orlando, others had no choice but to pursue other career paths. Nevertheless, the dependence on Russia was coming to an end with the SpaceX Falcon9 crewed launch that Saturday, which brought James a certain satisfaction.

After dinner, James scrolled through the news on his phone, which included ongoing protests over the death of George Floyd and declining COVID-19 deaths, though they might rise as more authorities process death certificates. At that moment, James received a call from his friend George.

"How's it going for the launch?" James asked. "Any problems?"

Ignoring the question, George said, "You're the physics guy. What's all this stuff about an alternate universe?" There is a logical reason George's fascination with UFOs had become focused on something else. The YouTube algorithms connected UFO searches with alternate universe subjects, and George had been viewing several videos on that topic.

Theoretical physics didn't align with James' field. He was more concerned with practical matters. He had several issues with the multi-universe idea, which he explained to George. In response, George pointed out the Mandela Effect. He was convinced that alternate universes were connected.

The Mandela Effect originated from paranormal researcher Fiona Broome, who claimed to have detailed memories of a news event in the 1980s. She recalled that South African anti-Apartheid leader Nelson Mandela had died in prison, but history tells a different story. Mandela survived prison, became President of South Africa from 1994 to 1999, and lived until 2013 in our universe. Nevertheless, many people shared the same memory of Mandela's "death," which Broome interpreted as evidence of a parallel universe.

George discovered that many people have false memories, leading some to consider them proof of alternate realities. These shared memories include instances like a painting of Henry VIII eating a turkey leg, which some recall seeing but no one can find a picture. Another example is a misquoted line from Snow White and the Seven Dwarfs. Even the geographic location of New Zealand is a subject of shared false memories. The list goes on, and it was once even the subject of an article in Good Housekeeping Magazine.

James remained unconvinced. He had a ready response: "Theories don't make footprints on the moon; it's math and science that puts them there." As he explained to George, there is no means to test the theory of alternate universes.

George needed to rest up to be ready for an early start of a launch the next day, so he left it there and said goodbye.

"You guys work all day and still want to 'talk shop'?" Judy asked. Judy had overheard the conversation and scoffed at the idea. She held the belief that Alternate Universes should be left to science fiction. James readily agreed.

It had been a hard week, so James spent a few minutes on his Mac laptop, skimming through email and a few social media posts, and called it a day. He said good night to Judy and went to bed early.

***

James slept peacefully that night, and as daylight peeked through the windows, he stumbled out of bed. As he stood, he heard a sound close to his ears, a whoosh reminiscent of Star Wars light sabers. His eyes widened as a glowing wave passed over him, like a ball of lightning forming a circle. He stumbled through the ring of light and felt startled when he discovered a wall  in front of him. Not only that, but the bedroom walls had changed from a soft beige to off-white. From the bed behind him, Judy was asking, "What's the matter? Did you forget how to find the bathroom?" Perhaps he HAD forgotten, or at least the bathroom wasn't where it should have been. Other things were different, too. The wood floor had turned into a brown shag carpet. He searched for the bathroom, contemplating the impossibility of the situation.

After James finished his shower, he found the bed made and Judy gone to the kitchen. He dressed and walked down the hall. The small kitchen reflected memories of the past: brown cabinets and a Formica countertop straight from the 1970s. He almost expected olive-green appliances, but they were all white.

Looking up from gently stirring a cup of frozen yogurt, Judy said, "It's about time you got going. We've got company today! Tommy is stopping on his way back to school."

James has a sense of panic. "Tommy?!" he asked blindly. He wondered almost out loud, *who is Tommy?* This was the same Judy, but everything else was different.

Judy's face showed a look of concern. "Yes, Tommy, our son, remember? Who did you think?" He would have to be more careful. Judy has always been very discerning. It was best not to raise her suspicions. It would be too much to explain, and she would certainly think he was crazy.

James opened several cupboard doors before finding an odd box of "organic" cereal. Next, he located a bowl, poured the cereal, and doused it with almond milk from the refrigerator. The house had an organic enclave vibe.

Sitting at the dining table, he glanced at the French doors leading to a patio and a fenced backyard. Turning back to Judy, he studied her carefully. She was the same Judy he had married, but the situation seemed all wrong.

The cool spring breeze of the morning air drifted into the room as Judy opened the outside door. An Irish Setter bounded into the room. The dog froze when he saw James and let out a low growl before moving toward him. James lowered the back of his hand toward the dog. The dog sniffed. Both James and the dog relaxed simultaneously. That was close, he thought. Had Judy noticed the dog's reaction?

After breakfast, James walked through the hallway as if touring an open house. At the end of the hall, he found a room set up as an office. He had not seen the need for a home office in his "other" life. His Apple laptop had been on a small table next to his favorite chair. But here, on the desk, was a cell phone resting on a wireless charger. As he picked it up and touched it, the face ID failed, going right to the passcode screen. After a few guesses, he gave up on the passcode. He spotted a pair of reading glasses on the desk. On a hunch, he put on the glasses and faced the phone again. This time, it worked! The phone responded, and he swiped to view the applications.

"Where am I?" he wondered. Opening Google Maps, he saw a red dot on a residential street north of Titusville. A satellite view showed the street and the surrounding neighborhood, typical of those developed in the early 1980s. The homes were mostly small, with a one-car garage. Many such homes were constructed under the FHA 235 program.

Sifting through the contacts on the phone, James was concerned when he did not find his close friend George at the Space Center.

He tapped the computer keyboard. The screen came to life, but unlike his faithful old Mac, it displayed the Windows logo. Luckily, the machine did not demand a password. He thought about some things George had said. On a hunch, he opened a browser and Google search for "Nelson Mandela." The first link on the page confirmed his suspicion. It included a reference to the death of Nelson Mandela while in prison in 1980. Contrary to his own knowledge, in this new reality, Nelson Mandela did not survive to become president of South Africa in later years.

James realized he had found himself in a different reality. Apprehension was creeping in.

In the world he had come from, COVID-19 was a big problem. But when he searched for that topic, he discovered the pandemic had been largely controlled. This current administration had used that research to control the virus by early February. The success, credited to the quick response by President Hillary Clinton?

How could that be?

But Hillary Clinton? President? What happened to all those emails and Benghazi?

It seems the CIA had uncovered Russia's actions behind Donald Trump. Trump's support had collapsed. COVID was gone, and Bill Clinton was now First Husband. Imagine that.

In the living room, James flipped on the TV. Moving through the channels, his attention landed on the Spanish channel, *Noticias Telemundo*. On the channel, he found a debate over an upcoming vote for Puerto Rico statehood.

Things were drastically different.

Judy stepped around the corner from the kitchen and asked, "Why are you watching that in Spanish?"

"Maybe I'm practicing my high school Spanish?" James replied. In high school, he had decided that Spanish would be a more practical choice than French, especially when visiting a foreign country, like Miami.

Judy's response was a curious mix of concern and surprise. "You never took Spanish in High School! You decided you wanted to be in my French class instead," she said as she returned to something she had been doing in the kitchen.

Judy possessed great intuition. She could often guess the plot of a movie and figure out *"whodunnit"* in the first few minutes. If she figured out what truly was going on, she might be more than a little upset. She might well have asked, "Who are you, and what have you done with my husband?" James needed to be careful not to let that happen.

He turned off the TV and continued exploring the house. Opening the back door from the kitchen, he was taken aback by the sight of a plug-in EV car in the garage.

As the doorbell rang, Judy went to the answer. James followed to join her at the door. A familiar-looking stranger stood before him.

"Hi, Dad! How's the new computer? When your old Mac died, I thought, it would a good time for a change. You can set up a password when you get used to it. Do you like your new office in my old room?"

This was Tommy, obviously James's son. He looked to be about nineteen. He was also tall, with his mother's eyes. Other than that, it was like seeing a younger version of himself. James had a strange feeling as he hugged his "new" son. At least, this would be a pleasant change to – whatever this experience was, he had found himself in.

James assumed his "new" son, Tommy, went to college somewhere. James had to be careful. He had many questions, but he had to pretend he knew all the answers.

Tommy reached out to bump fists with James and hugged his mom as he picked up a small stack of folded clothing Judy had ready for him. He waved goodbye as he drove away.

James had not quite recovered from that experience when Judy said, "I've got a surprise for you! We're meeting an old friend of yours for lunch!"

"Who is that?" he asked.

"I promised not to tell!" she said. "It's a surprise meeting. You'll see when we get there."

Disconnecting the charging cable from the car, James pushed the button to open the garage door. As he and Judy climbed in, he pushed the start button and backed out onto the street. He avoided using the car's navigation system because that might raise Judy's suspicions. James had a pretty good idea of the restaurant where the meeting was to take place. He used what he remembered from Google Maps to find his way out of the maze of the subdivision streets.

They got to the restaurant a bit early, and James tried to imagine who they might be meeting. As he glanced up from the menu, he thought he saw a ghost. The person walking toward their table bore a striking resemblance to his old friend, John. But it couldn't be John because he had died because of his alcoholism more than a year ago. James still felt the pain of losing his once closest friend.

James and Judy had both known John for a long time. They both blended well with musicians, and John had been a good one. John was a piano player and karaoke singer. Suffering through two failed marriages, John had become an alcoholic. Not that he didn't try to get it under control. He could go for months before dropping out of sight for a time, only to resurface later, as if nothing had happened. Everyone knew not to ask.

At one point, James was visiting John's home when he saw a bottle tucked into the corner of the room. Seeing the whiskey bottle had captured James's attention, John admitted, "That's going to kill me one day." His words had been prophetic. That day, James wanted to take away the bottle, but he failed to do so. He knew John would resent the interference, even from a friend. He reasoned John would only buy more, anyway. But James later comes to regret not taking the opportunity to show his friendship in that way.

Not long after, John called James. John said some things on that call that caused him concern. James knew the signs of suicidal depression. He had learned that from his NASA management training. At that moment, during John's call, James had wanted to go to John's house to talk some sense into him. But Judy had discouraged it. She reminded him there was nothing he could do. He should let John deal with his problems on his own, as he had done so many times before. It was true. John had often gone missing, only to resurface a week or so later. James had decided that Judy was probably right.

But that time had been very different. Not long after, John's brother called: the alcohol had taken its toll. They had moved John to hospice, where James and Judy went to see him for the last time. A catheter collected an ominous dark liquid at the foot of the bed. Everyone knew the dark liquid meant death was imminent. James found it hard to take. It was tough and very sad for everyone who cared for John. James could not bring himself to go to the funeral. He regretted not going to John's rescue when he had the chance too much.

But now, here was John! Very much alive and standing there, happy and well! John had dark features and stood about five feet tall. His hair was balding in the center. At a distance, he might be mistaken for George Costanza from the old Seinfeld show. John wore a white short-sleeved button shirt and gray slacks—his typical nightclub wardrobe. John was never one for wearing jeans.

There was a woman with John, but younger. Her face showed the signs of a hard life, topped by hair that was a ... hmm, tasteful shade of purple, tied in a ponytail. In contrast to John, she wore jeans, or the jeans were wearing her. It wasn't easy to tell.

"I can't thank you enough for saving my life!" John said. "You were a genuine friend when I hit bottom, and you convinced me to get my life together. I didn't want to, but you made me promise to join AA, and, well, I did it. It's still a struggle, but I made it! " turning to the woman next to him, "Well, we made it together. Oh, I want you to meet Pat! She was my AA sponsor, and, well, we have a lot in common."

Pat leaned in to shake hands with James and touched his shoulder. "I'm so glad to meet you, Jim!"

John corrected, "He prefers James." James once explained the reason to John. James has a certain dignity. James always thought that was why it was James Bond and James Thurber, not Jim Bond and Jim Thurber.

"Oh, I'm sorry, James! We're both glad you were such a good friend to John," Pat added.

"I can't go back to working at the club," John continued. "Pat warned me to stay far away from the booze. I need to remember I'll always be a recovering alcoholic. So I'm going to be a music teacher! I'll be working at a music store, and Pat will help me find students. We even made some YouTube videos! No more nightclubs! Can you imagine that? And I owe it all to you... and to Pat, of course!"

James glanced at Judy, her smile filled with tears of happiness. "I knew you would want to know about John's success!" she said.

He tried to hold back the tears of joy, which rolled over him like an ocean wave.

"John, that's so great!" Pat said. "It's so good to see you. We couldn't be happier for you. You did it. You should be proud of yourself."

Changing the subject, James interrupted, "So, what will you have? We like roast beef sandwiches here, but the fried chicken is also pretty good! Come on, let's go order at the counter."

It had been a beautiful reunion. The four talked well past finishing the meal before saying their goodbyes.

Back in the car, James told Judy, "That was a wonderful surprise. It was so nice to see what John has accomplished. I think he's going to make it now. He and Pat are clearly helping each other."

What a day it had been, and so much to absorb and sort out. In this alternative universe, this new dimension, he now had a son, and his old friend had come back from the dead.

At home, James slipped into a comfortable chair, scanning a few YouTube videos on his phone. The news channels hyped up some big announcements that Monday. Jimmy Carter and President Hillary Clinton (?) would make an important announcement.

What? Carter? Why Jimmy Carter? Hillary had promised in her campaign to find out the truth about UFOs, and James remembered that Jimmy Carter had said he had seen a flying saucer. Was that connected? James curiously wondered what they might say, but he was sure George would love it. That is, if George existed in this strange alternative universe. There was no contact listed for George on his phone. Had he gained one friend only to lose another?

Shifting back to reality, one thing could present a serious challenge. Where would he go to work on Monday? He had one day to figure that out, with not much to go on. Where would he go?

What if this alternate James Cooper he had replaced had a job that this James knew nothing about?

What if he couldn't pull it off?

What if Judy couldn't accept an alternate husband if she learned the truth? And what would happen to the Judy in the other universe he left behind? How would she cope? How would she survive? She would report surely him missing, and his job at NASA would be history, in more than one sense, if he weren't there to show up on Monday.

But how could it all be possible? The concept of multiple universes, of parallel realities, of course, remained only a theory. James was certain of that, or at least he had been. Would he be stuck in this parallel universe? Would the other James Cooper appear? What would he do if he met his other self? Could that even be possible? He wasn't sure about anything anymore. Impossible thoughts filled his mind. He tried a Google Search for "Alternate Universes." It produced a link to a TED Talk YouTube video. The video featured a "famous" Princeton physics professor, Cedric Clark, whom James had never heard of.

Professor Clark's presentation title was "Sine Wave Theory of Creation." The professor had deduced that there could be no alternate universes. His reason was that it would follow that no single body of matter could occupy more than one space at a time. It made sense so far... In the video, Clark also asserted that the universe is infinite, not finite. He posed the question, *if you were to reach the end of a finite universe, what would be beyond that? A wall?* The professor's corollary held that for the same reason, the Big Bang could not be a singular event but one small part of a continuing cycle. The Big Bang would only serve as a zero point in one cycle of infinite expansions and contractions.

That was all well and good as a theory, but if parallel universes can't exist, what would explain this current situation?

James silenced his phone and put it on charge. His mind swirled with conflicting ideas, questions, and contradictions as he later drifted off to sleep.

***

James awoke and opened his eyes. As he scanned the room, he was relieved to find the bathroom door where it belonged, and the walls were again the right color. He found himself back in his old bedroom!

It had all been a dream! Relieved that nothing had changed, he let out a deep sigh and went to take a shower.

As he dressed, he noticed a pleasant aroma from the kitchen. Judy was baking homemade biscuits.

"Fresh-baked biscuits on a Saturday? What's the occasion?" James asked.

"Today is Sunday!" she said with a quizzical expression. "Are you alright?"

"Sorry! I thought it was Saturday," James responded as he tried to make sense of things all over again. How could he have missed an entire day? He felt an icy shiver sweeping over him with the realization that perhaps he might not have been dreaming after all.

He swallowed hard, almost choking on the biscuit, when he noticed Judy studying his face. She quickly turned away as he looked up. Had she noticed something to cause suspicion?

"Will you be seeing John this week?" she said with a look of concern.

The question startled James. He hesitated. "Don't you remember?" John passed away from alcoholism last year."

Judy remained still for a moment before she replied, "Oh … That's right. It's hard to believe he's gone. I almost feel like I saw him yesterday…" Her words trailed off.

James watched as she removed the dishes and silverware from the dishwasher. She opened several cupboards and drawers, as if trying to decide where things should go. Judy appeared to be concerned or worried about something.

"What's your schedule at the store this week?" James inquired. As branch manager, Judy often had to fill in for employees who had to take time off. He was surprised she wasn't scheduled to work that weekend.

Judy hesitated before answering, "My normal schedule, I think…" She went to a small work desk in the hall past the kitchen, and began sifting through the contents of a drawer until she found a small calendar with notes in the squares for the days.

"Do you need to stop by the office today to check with Ann?" James asked. Judy's Assistant Manager worked the weekends.

"I don't think so," Judy answered quickly. Pausing, she said, "I think we need to do some grocery shopping."

As James settled into a chair in the living room and began sorting through his phone messages, Judy announced, "Let's go to the store. Would you like to drive?"

James nodded as he got up from the chair and went to grab his wallet and keys from the bedroom.

Later, James followed as Judy began making her selections in the store. She stopped at the dairy case and extracted a bottle of sugar-free almond milk. A thought flowed over James like a splash of icy water. Her selection appeared starkly out of character, but it was exactly what the "other" Judy might have done.

His mind swirled with possibilities and options, but he said nothing.

As they drove from the store, James stole a quick glance at Judy as she gazed at the scenery. It was as if she was taking mental notes of the route and landmarks. Could he be imagining things? But what could explain the uncharacteristic selections at the grocery store? Could he test his suspicions without the danger of spilling a giant cauldron of cosmic beans?

James began his strategy by asking, "Have you ever thought about how things might have turned out if we had made different decisions along the way?" He paused, "I mean, we could have had children, we could have lived in a different place, we could have chosen different jobs."

He continued, "You know how George is all about science fiction and the space alien rumors. Lately, George has been talking about the idea of a parallel universe and alternate realities. He thinks there might be multiple versions of us living different lives in different dimensions."

Judy squirmed in her seat as she listened. "What if there could be another version of us where we have a child?"

Judy paused, and it appeared there was something she wanted to say, but decided against it. She continued to process the words and nodded slowly. "I suppose it's possible, but it's still very hard to believe."

James knew he had to tread cautiously. "I know it's a lot to take in, but I think it's worth considering. It could explain a lot of the strange things that have been happening lately."

Judy's eyes widened again, and as James glanced over at her, he could see a strange look in her eyes as she began to speak, but stopped short.

She remained silent for a moment, and James could see the tears forming in her eyes. "I don't understand what is happening," she breathed, but did not explain further.

When they returned to the house, they began unloading the groceries. Soon, they unloaded the groceries, put them away, and folded the paper bags for recycling.

Turning to James, Judy glanced at him and said, "I have a confession." I'm not who you think I am."

The words reverberated in James's ear, his thoughts racing. He had it all figured out—he would explain what he had experienced, and now... this...

James asked, "What do you mean?"

"When I woke up this morning, I didn't know where I was, but I looked across the bed and saw you. You were there, but everything seemed different. The house and the view from the window are all changed. I had to look in the mirror to be sure I was still me. I don't know if I can deal with it all."

James took a deep breath and turned to Judy, trying to decide how to respond. "I want you to know I believe you. And I want you to know that you are still the best thing that ever happened to me, no matter what universe we're in."

James spoke softly. "I have my own confession to make. I've been to that other universe. It was yesterday. But this morning I woke up back here. You must have passed through the same portal."

Judy looked as if struck with an electric shock as she quickly sat down on the comforting, soft living room couch, slowly dealing with what she heard.

"I don't know how it's possible, but it happened," James says, still trying to wrap his head around the experience. "I was in your universe on Saturday, and I woke up back here today, Sunday."

Now Judy's mind raced with the possibilities. "Did you see me? Did you see Tommy? And John?" she asked,

"Yes," James assured her.

Judy was trying hard to take it all in. "What can we do?"

"I'm not sure we can do anything. I mean, we don't know how it happened or why." James continued, "I mean, it's impossible in so many ways, but now…"

Judy assured him, "I believe everything happens for a reason. "

James nodded in agreement. "I'll see if I can find any research about this," he says. "In the meantime, we should try not to draw attention to our - situation."

Judy nodded, staring ahead, still processing everything. Judy took a moment to let everything sink in. "But what does that mean for us now? Are we both stuck in this universe forever?" she asks, feeling a sense of unease.

"Okay. We'll figure this out together," James said as he placed a reassuring hand on Judy's arm.

Judy smiled in agreement. She turned toward James, leaned forward, and whispered. "You can start by telling me where the heck I go to work tomorrow."

James's phone rang. It was George. Nineteen hours after the launch of the new SpaceX Crew Dragon, the newly arrived astronauts passed through the DM-2 hatch to enter the ISS. George completed his task and wanted to share the experience with James. There was a launch delay earlier in the week because of the weather, but everything went as planned this time. George and his team had made history. As the two spoke, Judy whispered, "Who is George?" James waved his hand and mouthed the words, "I'll explain later."

After the call, James smiled at Judy as he spoke. "George is a wonderful friend. He's a part of the history of KSC, the Space Center, and NASA. I got to know him after, you know, I lost John.

Judy smiled understandingly and began to say something, but James stopped her. "George must never know. NASA might overlook rumors about space aliens. But this?" he shook his head as she said, "John was a wonderful person and a good friend. Now I understand how you reacted to seeing him."

James paused for a moment before he continued. "George has a lot of strange ideas. He talks about space aliens a lot, although recently he had been talking about alternate universes."

Judy took a breath, and she was going to speak, but James stopped her.

"George must never know. NASA might overlook rumors about space aliens. But this?" he shook his head. George talks to EVERY-BODY!"

Judy was concerned. "What will happen to Tommy? We are going to miss so much!"

"For all we know, there's another version of us back in his world looking after him. He'll be fine," James assured her. "But I'm sure glad I got to meet him, even if only for a short time."

Judy agreed. "I'm glad you did, too."

Now it was time for James to satisfy his curiosity. He asked Judy, "What job did I have?"

"It had something to do with communications. You always had to work crazy hours because of the rocket launches." To James, it sounded a lot like George's job. That might explain why he had not found George in the phone contacts. Was it possible James was hired instead of George? That made sense. If James had not gone on to earn his physics degree, he would not have qualified to be the rocket scientist he is now.

Judy explained James had wanted to continue to graduate school for a degree in physics, but ... then Tommy happened.

***

The next morning, James gazed around the room in the dim morning light to assure himself that nothing had changed from the night before. He glanced over to Judy's side of the bed, where she lay sleeping soundly. They had talked about her job, her position as manager, and where she would need to go that morning. Hopefully, they could adjust to a new "normal." He had to be at the office by 8, but she could enjoy a few more minutes of sleep. After all, she had been through a lot in the last few days. They both had. But she would have a bit more adjustments to make than he would. He showered and dressed as quietly as possible.

Judy stirred awake. "What time is it?", she asked as she glanced at the clock on the nightstand. "I need to get going. Ann worked the weekend, so I won't have her to fall back on this morning." She got up and went about her business, getting ready for the day.

As James entered the kitchen, Judy pulled the almond milk from the refrigerator. "What's this about?" she asked.

James stammered... "We... bought it... yesterday..." Judy's face grimaced as she poured a small amount into a glass and sipped it. "It's not bad, but I certainly wouldn't have bought it."

Was she playing tricks on him? What had happened? James now had a new shock to recover from. He had just gotten used to the reality of a "new" Judy, and now this. In fact, he had fallen in love all over again. But somehow, during the night, the "other" Judy had slipped back into this reality.

James must have been thinking this wasn't a portal so much as it was becoming a revolving door!

There was no time to sort it out, it was time to get to their respective jobs. James would have to resist the urge to discuss the topic with George, but Judy would be back at her old routine, perhaps wondering what she had "dreamed" over the weekend if, indeed, she thought about it at all. It's only a dream! After all, that's what he had thought it when he found himself in another existence.

But ... what if she shared her "dream" experience with him? What would he say? How would he explain it? What if she was jealous of her "other" self? After all, James could not deny that he had fallen in love with her all over again, which would be a truly weird feeling to have.

James concluded that in the same way, the two versions of Judy had traveled between alternate universes, it became logical to believe that his other self had taken the trip in reverse. How would the Judy from yesterday react to being back where she had been after she had almost adjusted to a second reality? Would any of them be able to maintain their sanity? More, could they keep the secret?

But what if....

***

While the concept of parallel or multiple universes has been the subject of scientific debate for more than a century, interest in the concept has increased in recent years. For example, where is "Heaven" if not in a parallel universe?

But this story is not really about science. It is about decisions, our own decisions, and the decisions of others. Some decisions might even affect history. We never know. When those decisions arise, we must ask ourselves...

What if?

The Time the Aliens Came

After almost thirty years of teaching, Mildred Jenkins retired on her pension from the Leon County School District. She spent most of her evenings with her knitting and her cat, named Fred. After the weekly newspaper shut down, the local folks down at the Little Dollar store said it didn't matter, as they had Mildred. She naturally kept tabs on what was happening in the neighborhood.

That's when it happened. It began late one summer night in July as Mildred saw a strange light coming through the trees outside her window. She put down her knitting and nudged the cat from her lap. She got up from the large leather armchair to take a look, pulling back the curtains on the window.

The lights seemed to come from the lakefront cabin next door. There shouldn't be anyone there this time of year, Mildred thought. The cabin was the winter home of Evelyn Montgomery, but she always left in April for her summer home in North Carolina, as did several others in the small north Florida community. Mildred listened closely to see if it might be a car, but the only sounds she heard were crickets and the occasional call of the Whippoorwill. She watched as the lights reflected off the trees, and then, without a sound, they quickly faded away. "That's strange!" she thought, watching for a few moments more. But there was nothing more to see.

10:23 pm. Mildred made a note of the time on a pad she had on the coffee table for such occasions. Fred, the cat, had claimed the seat in the big gray chair. Mildred let him be and decided it was time for bed.

***

The next morning, Mildred peeked through the shades in her bedroom to see if anything was going on at the house next door, but everything appeared quiet. At least, so it seemed. She decided to check with Sherry Green across the road in case Sherry had noticed anything that night.

"Hello, Mildred," Mrs. Green answered the phone, apparently noting the name on the Caller I.D.

"Hi, Sherry," Mildred replied. "Did you see anything unusual last night, about 10:30 or so?"

Sherry perked up at the possibility of some excitement in the dull little village. "Oh, did I miss something? An accident? Or a burglary?" she said with some concern in her voice.

"No, nothing like that. I only wondered if you saw a strange light in the woods about that time. It swooped in over the trees without a sound. And then it was gone."

"What do you suppose it could be?" Sherry asked.

"Well, I can't say," Mildred responded. "I had hoped you might have seen it. Oh, well. Thanks anyway."

Later, at the Little Dollar store, Henry Thompson, the store manager, rang up an order for Agnes Patterson, another retiree who lived within walking distance of the store.

"Did you hear what happened last night?" Agnes asked Mr. Thompson. Apparently, Sherry Green had called Agnes about what Mildred had told her earlier that morning. Word had already been spreading through the community.

Mr. Thompson continued ringing up the sale. "Would you like the receipt?" he asked, seemingly ignoring the question.

"No, I don't need a receipt, thank you. Mildred said she saw some strange lights in the sky near her house last night." Sherry continued, loud enough so more people in the store could hear.

Tommy Jones, the stock clerk, spoke up. "I bet it's them!" he said.

"Them who?" Turning his head with a grimace, Mr. Thompson directed his question to Tommy.

Tommy, in his early twenties, sported a short beard and shaggy hair, combed to reveal one pierced earring. He mainly worked in the stockroom of the Little Dollar store.

"Them aliens!", he said. "I've been hearing about them a lot on the news," he said confidently. By *the news*", Tommy meant YouTube and Facebook.

***

An enterprising woman in her early fifties, Janet Taylor had one of only two real estate offices in the area. Everyone knew Janet Taylor for her attention to detail. As a real estate broker, she managed vacation rental properties for the owners, many of whom were not full-time residents. Being observant was in her nature.

She was returning from a rental property she managed when she passed by Mildred's house. As she rounded the corner, she thought she saw something or someone behind Evelyn Montgomery's cabin. It was hard to see as she concentrated on negotiating the bends in the road. At first glance, though, whatever it was had large dark eyes and what could have been a helmet. She couldn't stop to investigate because she was late for an appointment at the office.

Back at the real estate office, Agnes Patterson waited patiently in her car outside the small office. She had been considering renting out the cottage where her mother had lived before her death earlier that year.

Janet pulled into her reserved spot and unlocked the office door.

"Good afternoon, Agnes," greeted warmly. "As I mentioned on the phone, I believe a seasonal rental could be a wonderful option for you. There's a demand for charming cottages in the area, especially during the winter months. As you know, I manage several rental properties in the area."

Agnes leaned forward attentively. "What do you think I can expect in terms of income for the winter months?"

"Well, Agnes, based on the current rental market and the appeal of your cottage's location, I think you can expect something in this range." Janet pointed to the prices on a rental list she had on her desk.

"That's more than I expected. Go ahead and fill out the forms, and I'll stop by later to sign them." Agnes was relieved. She still had expenses that were left over from her mother's illness, and the rental income would be a big help.

Changing the subject, Agnes asked, "Did you hear about the strange lights out by Mildred Jenkin's house last night? I stopped by the Little Dollar store and everybody was talking about it."

"You know, I passed by there this morning after showing a rental, and I thought I saw something at the Montgomery cabin," Janet replied. "Something or someone with big eyes creeping around through the bushes."

Agnes was concerned. "Do you think we should call Mike?" Mike Reynolds was the local deputy. The town was not big enough for a real police department, so the county assigned a deputy to patrol the area. In view of the discussion at the store, the girls thought it might be a good idea to ask Mike to check out the stranger Janet had seen in the woods.

As Agnes left and headed home, Janet decided to share her concerns with the local deputy sheriff. With a determined sigh, she picked up her phone and dialed the number for the sheriff's office. "Sheriff's office, Deputy Reynolds speaking," a calm and professional voice answered on the other end of the line.

"Hello, Mike, this is Janet Taylor," she began. "I wanted to bring something to your attention. People all over town have been talking about the space aliens up at the Montgomery house by the lake."

Deputy Reynolds paused for a moment, taking in the information. "Space aliens? At the Montgomery house?" he replied, sounding slightly surprised. "I haven't heard anything about that."

"Yes, everybody's talking about it," she explained, trying to convey the seriousness of the situation. "I know it sounds ridiculous, but that's what they're saying down at the Little Dollar Store."

"I understand, Janet," the deputy said in a reassuring tone. "Well, I guess it's my duty to investigate any reports that might affect the community's well-being."

"Thank you, Mike," she said, feeling relieved that the deputy was willing to listen.

"I appreciate you letting me know," Deputy Reynolds replied. "I'll look into it and see what is going on."

Janet was grateful for the deputy's assurance. "You'll be sure to let me know what you find out, won't you?"

"I will, Janet, and thank you for bringing this to my attention," the deputy said sincerely.

"I'll leave it in your capable hands, Mike," she replied, feeling grateful the deputy was taking her concerns seriously.

She decided to stop by the Little Dollar store to find out what everybody was talking about.

As Janet was picking up a few things from the back of the store, Tommy Jones was refilling the coolers with dairy products. "How are you today, Ms. Taylor?" he asked. "Have you heard about the space aliens out at the Montgomery place last night?"

"I was by there this morning, and I saw something creepy in the woods. I called the deputy and asked him to check it out," she replied.

"I think it's them aliens," Tommy said with a look of certainty. "It's been all over the news, you know."

Ten-year-old Emily Campbell was visiting with her grandmother for the summer. She had heard the discussion from the end of the next aisle. She stepped out of the aisle and turned to look at Tommy with her hands on her hips. "Seriously? You think it's space, people?" she said with a look of disgust. Her grandmother promptly silenced her, unwilling to let the young girl come across as impolite. Emily resisted but soon folded her hands and rejoined her grandmother in the paper goods aisle.

"Mr. Thompson? Is it OK if I go on break now?" Tommy asked. Mr. Thompson waved his hand, indicating his approval.

Tommy slipped into the side stockroom and started texting.

Tommy: "Hey, Sandy, you won't believe what I've been hearing at work! There's this stranger staying in the woods, and people are saying they saw lights like UFOs! #AlienAlert"

Sandra : "OMG, this sounds like something out of a sci-fi movie! "

Tommy: "I think the aliens have landed, like we've been hearing on the news. It's wild! I'm gonna text Joey to find out what he's heard. SYL."

Tommy to Joey: "Did you hear about the spaceship in the woods up by the Montgomery place?"

Joey : "No, what's up with that?"

Tommy: "People in the store are saying there might be space aliens wandering in the woods down by the lake."

Joey: "Did anyone see the spaceship?"

Tommy: "Mildred Jenkins said she saw a spaceship land

right before midnight. Sherry Green said she saw a creature with big eyes creeping through the palmettos this morning"

Joey: "Somebody should call the sheriff!"

Tommy: "I think somebody did report it to the sheriff. Gotta go. Mr. Thompson is probably wondering what I'm doing."

***

As Deputy Mike Reynolds cautiously approached the Montgomery cabin, Mildred waved him closer.

"Hi, Mildred. Say! Janet Taylor thought she saw someone creeping about at Evelyn's place. Have you noticed anything over there?"

Mildred cocked her head to one side as she thought. "Now that you mention it, my cat, Fred, acted a little strange when I let him out this morning. I told Sherry Green I saw some lights in the woods last night."

At that moment, a twig cracked, breaking in back of the old cabin next door. Deputy Reynolds adjusted his gun belt and gave a side salute to Mildred as he turned to investigate.

Mike moved quietly to the side of the house. Peeking through the azalea bush, he saw the "creature" Janet described, with what looked like large dark eyes on the top of its head, stooping next to a palmetto.

As the deputy moved closer, he shouted out, "Hello?"

"Hello! Is there a problem?" was the reply, as the "creature" stood up, revealing a gray sun hat with wrap-around sunglasses perched on top. It was easy to see how that combination, from a distance, would resemble the classic alien's head when looking down.

"Can I ask who you are and what you are doing here?" Deputy Mike asked the stranger.

The "stranger" was an older gentleman wearing denim coveralls. In one hand, he held a small bowl containing saw palmetto berries. He reached out his other hand to the deputy.

"I'm Dr. George Montagu. I'm a professor at the College of Agriculture in Gainesville. Evelyn Montgomery's daughter is one of my students. She's allowing me to stay at their cabin while I conduct some research on the effects of climate change on the edible berries in this area, specifically the Saw Palmetto. But why are you here, if I might ask?"

The deputy stroked his cheek and looked up at the trees as he thought about how to respond. "The neighbors said they noticed some strange lights in the sky late last night, but they didn't hear any sound, so it couldn't have been a car. Would you know anything about that?"

"That would be about the time Evelyn's daughter dropped me off last night. Her car is electric, so it wouldn't make any sounds," the professor explained.

The deputy shook his head. "Well, that explains it. But you have no idea what's been going around. The folks down at the Little Dollar had it figured out that the aliens had landed here. The neighbors saw the lights, someone else saw your sunglasses on your head through the bushes, and well, one thing led to another…"

The two of them had a nice laugh, and then the deputy asked, "Do you think we should tell them or just let them think the aliens came here for a visit?"

The Camera That Saw Through Time

Ethan confidently pointed to a camera in the display case. "I want THAT one, please."

A curious and imaginative teenager, Ethan had a natural passion for photography. In his small English village, he discovered a charming old second-hand store. Thirteen-year-old Ethan, always nurturing a special love for photography, delighted in finding a display of cameras. 

The store clerk reached into the case to retrieve the camera and hand it to the boy.

As Alex examined the camera, turning it around to reveal the brand name, he said, "I've never heard of Vixtel." He looked to the clerk for a response, but the clerk raised his eyebrows and turned his head with an expression that meant he didn't have an answer. It was in a second-hand store, after all. It could have come from anywhere.

"It must be special," Ethan said. He was startled by what he saw as he switched the camera on. Through the camera's lens, the old store looked different. Ethan pointed the camera around the store. The digital screen revealed vivid colors and made some of the old things on the store shelves look almost new. He checked the menu functions, but there was no HDR or High Dynamic Range setting, which might have explained the brilliant colors.

Ethan convinced himself that this magical camera was exactly what he wanted. Checking the tag, he found a pleasant surprise. The price matched the amount he had in his pocket! He smiled and handed his money to the clerk, completing the deal.

"Here," said the clerk, "it comes with a case and a few lens filters."

"Thank you," said Ethan.

Ethan rode his bicycle home as the late afternoon shadows hovered over the narrow streets of the old village. Summer filled the air, and school being out meant he would have plenty of time to explore with his new camera.

***

The following day, Ethan began his adventure, exploring his world with the magical camera. He rode his bicycle into the village, looking for subjects to photograph. He stopped at an ancient bridge that spanned a serene river. As he framed the scene and pressed the shutter, the display changed before his eyes, revealing a happy family in a horse-drawn carriage. Ethan moved the camera away from his face, but the people and the carriage were nowhere to be seen. The camera had transported him into another era. But how could that be?

Ethan crossed the bridge into the village as he wondered about the possibilities. Ahead, an old cathedral dominated the town square with its towering spires. As he paused to snap a picture, the walls transformed inside the camera, washing away the years of dirt and fading. Intricate carvings and ornate patterns came to life. The camera revealed the hidden beauty, no longer burdened by the weight of time. The stained-glass windows glowed with vibrant hues of color in the morning sunlight. Ethan parked his bicycle and walked through the giant open doorway to the sanctuary. He raised his camera, framed the scene from the entrance, and pressed the shutter. The photograph captured not only the physical attributes of the cathedral but also the spirit of its rich history. Ethan spent much of the next hour capturing scenes of the cathedral's beauty from different perspectives. He snapped the shutter as he crouched below the towering majesty of the organ pipes and climbed the stairs to capture a view of the pulpit and choir benches from the balcony. Through the camera's display, Ethan studied how the windows cast their colors on the aisles below. He snapped close-ups of the ornate carvings of the church benches. As he set the focus and the f-stop to a narrow field of view, the images took on the appearance of three dimensions. Ethan felt pure excitement for the art of photography, limited only by the perspective of the camera's single prime lens.

As Ethan emerged from the cathedral, he looked around to see what else he might explore with the magical camera. An elderly woman sat resting on a bench beside the fountain in the town square.

"Excuse me," he asked, "may I take your picture?"

The old woman's weathered face, punctuated with wise eyes, studied Ethan curiously as the young boy stood before her. At last, she parsed her lips as if to show he had passed her inspection. "Why would you want to do that?" she asked.

Ethan considered a respectful response. "Um, excuse me. You being here makes this place look even better. It's like you bring something special to the scene. Can I take a photo to capture this moment? It would mean a lot to me."

The woman nodded in solemn agreement. "I'm not inclined to pose, you know," she said firmly.

"I'm not inclined to ask," Ethan responded as he began exploring different angles and settings on the lens. "I think you will like what you see."

Ethan took several minutes to find the right composition for each scene. He took one close-up study of the woman's face with the defocused fountain in the background. In another, he framed the woman on the bench in perspective against the sidewalk and trees stretching off into the distance. At one point, a curious squirrel came to visit, and Ethan captured the woman's expression as she greeted the young creature. In another shot, Ethan positioned the camera so that the sun splashed across the lens with a streak of light.

The camera's display screen revealed what the camera had captured. The wrinkles of age on the woman's face softened, as if the hands of time were rewinding. The woman looked on in wonder and amazement as Ethan showed her the pictures. "How did you do that?" she asked almost defiantly.

"My camera can see the beauty that's inside. It captures what makes you, well, you. When I take pictures with this camera, I can save the beautiful scenes and the special people that make the world awesome." Ethan explained, trying his best to express his thoughts. "It's like a magic window to keep the good stuff from slipping away."

The woman listened, not fully accepting the reality of the situation. Still, she expressed her gratitude to Ethan for bringing her the special moment of her day. She thanked him as he placed the cover on the lens, put the camera back inside the case, and climbed on his bike to continue on his way.

***

As Ethan walked his bike along the path in the park, he encountered a young couple posing for a professional photographer. Ethan stood at a distance, observing the scene as the photographer directed the couple to various poses and adjusted the camera. Upon completing his work and thanking the couple, he packed up his equipment. The older man sported a well-groomed salt-and-pepper beard with wavy chestnut hair, also neatly styled. He appeared tall and confident, dressed in a tailored charcoal gray suit. Next to him, a weathered leather camera bag stood open, housing an expensive camera case nestled alongside an assortment of lens cases. A large box of reflectors and tripods stood open to one side.

Ethan found the courage to approach the photographer. "I see you have a camera," the man said. "You must be a photographer, too!"

"I would really like to be one day," Ethan answered. "I've been trying out my new camera."

The photographer stood straight and peered over his glasses at Ethan. "Let's see what you have."

Ethan turned on the camera and stepped through the images he had captured.

"These are quite remarkable!" he exclaimed to Ethan's proud satisfaction.

"I think it's a magical camera."

"Do you think so?" said the photographer. "I see some genuine talent in your pictures." He reached into his top pocket and retrieved a business card: Alex "Lex" Montgomery, Wedding Photographer, it said. "I'm Lex. What might be your name?" he asked.

The young boy reached up to shake his hand. "I'm Ethan," he answered.

"You keep taking pictures like these, and I'm going to have some serious competition," said Alex with a grin.

Ethan thanked Alex as he said goodbye.

He wanted to take one last picture before heading home. As the afternoon sun painted streaks of color in the sky, he carefully placed his camera on a park table and attached a neutral density filter. He set the camera and the lens for a long exposure. The people in the park scurried about, gathering up various children and their toys as the evening approached. Others strolled along the pathways and stopped to take in the sunset's beauty. The camera clicked, marking the end of the exposure. The camera's display screen revealed streaks where people had been moving about. In the foreground, a couple stood holding hands, taking in the sun sinking into the horizon.

Ethan rode his bike home as darkness fell. He leaned his bike against a tree and went inside. His mother complained he had missed supper, but Ethan hurried upstairs. He thought, "Dinner can wait," as he moved the pictures from the camera to his school laptop.

***

That night, Ethan dreamed of new things he could do with the magical camera, envisioning new subjects and techniques. The next day, he awoke early, all but gulping down the croissant his mother had made for his breakfast before rushing back up the stairs to his room. He seized his faithful camera and set out to find more adventures.

Once again, his bicycle tires thumped across the stones of the old bridge into the village, his camera safely wrapped in a cloth in the bicycle basket.

Bump! As Ethan was looking for something to photograph, the bike hit a large root in the road, causing the camera to tumble to the ground. He scooped it up to inspect it for damage. Relieved to find no cracks or scratches, he carefully wrapped it again and continued on his way.

Riding his bicycle into the village, he came across a small farm. "This might be a nice subject for pictures," he thought. He peeked through the fence and saw a tiny baby lamb in the farmyard. Ethan quietly braced himself against the rough boards of the fence, following the little animal with his camera and taking several pictures as the cute baby lamb jumped and pranced about. While reviewing the images, he felt proud to capture the pure joy of the little lamb at play, momentarily forgetting about the camera's magical abilities.

Ethan peddled into the village, intent on finding more subjects for his camera adventures. He turned a corner to see the rotting structure of an old water-powered gristmill. Ethan thought, "I wonder how it looked when it was new?" He reached for the camera in its wrapping and switched it on. As he focused on the old building, it looked ... ordinary! The camera's magic powers to reveal the past had vanished. It must have happened when the camera fell out of the bicycle basket. Ethan felt devastated!

Reaching into his pocket, he found the card the photographer in the park gave him. Perhaps the magic could be restored! Bundling the camera into the bicycle basket, Ethan found his way to the address on the card. The photographer's shop was a storefront on the main road. As he glanced through the glass, Ethan saw Alex speaking with the young couple from the park. They were likely reviewing the wedding pictures from the day before. As the couple left the store with their wedding album, Alex looked up to see Ethan and beckoned for him to come in.

"Hello! What brings you here today?" he asked the clearly sad Ethan.

Ethan explained that his camera once had magical qualities, revealing the brilliance of the old cathedral and the youthful image of the old woman in the park. But now, the magic was gone.

"Can you find the settings? Can you fix it?" he pleaded.

The older man smiled knowingly. "There's nothing wrong with the settings, he told Ethan. "The magic is real, but it is in your imagination. You have discovered the possibilities within yourself and the many things you can do with the camera. Your imagination gives the camera its ability to create the magic in the images you can create."

As Alex shared his wisdom with Ethan, the young photographer's eyes widened with a newfound understanding. "You mean, the magic in my camera is actually my own imagination and my growing skill in using it?" Ethan questioned, seeking confirmation.

Alex smiled warmly, nodding in agreement. "Exactly, Ethan. The camera is simply a tool, but the real magic lies within you. It's your unique perspective, your creativity, and your passion that breathes life into every photograph you take."

Ethan's face lit up with a mixture of excitement and realization. "So, it's not about freezing moments, but about capturing the emotions and memories that touch people's hearts?"

Alex nodded again, his eyes filled with pride. "Absolutely! Photography has the power to evoke emotions, to tell stories, and to preserve precious memories. It's your own vision, your ability to see beauty in the world, that creates the magic. With every click of the shutter, you have the power to make the world a little more beautiful, one frame at a time."

Ethan's mind raced with possibilities, his imagination ignited by the empowering words of the experienced photographer. "I see it now, Alex. It's not about the camera but about the magic I can create through my own vision and creativity. I can make a difference with my photographs."

Alex beamed with pride, a mentor's satisfaction emanating from his being. "That's the spirit, Ethan! Never forget that the true magic of photography lives within you. Embrace your unique perspective, explore your creativity, and keep capturing the beauty surrounding us. Your vision has the power to touch hearts and make the world a better place."

With newfound clarity, Ethan understood his camera had been merely a conduit for his imagination and artistic expression. The true magic lay within himself, waiting to be unlocked with every frame he captured. As he thanked Alex for the invaluable lesson, Ethan walked away, fueled by a renewed sense of purpose and the knowledge that he could create his own magic, one photograph at a time.

We Saw the Aliens

“ A shley Taylor reporting from Oceanside Beach, where there were several reports earlier this evening of a strange light in the sky. One report said that they saw what looked like a bright light hovering over the ocean and disappeared. We contacted the local airport, but they had no reports of a missing plane and no radar reports of anything unusual in the area. Still, local witnesses insist they saw something out there.” She turned to point out to sea to her left as the news camera switched back to the studio.

(Earlier that evening...)

Lisa and Mark strolled hand in hand along the moonlit beach, their laughter mingling with the gentle crashing of the waves. The cool breeze kissed their faces as they relished the moment's intimacy, oblivious to the world around them. As they gazed into each other's eyes, a sudden burst of blinding light above shattered their tender moment. As  their attention drawn toward the light, their eyes widened with a mix of curiosity and awe.

“Holy... What IS that?” Mark exclaimed, his voice tinged with excitement and disbelief.

Lisa's heart skipped a beat as her gaze followed Mark's, fixating on the mysterious object hovering in the night sky. It seemed to defy all reason, an otherworldly presence that had intruded upon their romantic moment.

"Is that... what I think it is?" she murmured, her voice barely audible.

They watched, transfixed, as a sizeable disk-shaped object hovered over the water at some distance offshore. Its metallic surface shimmered with an ethereal glow as it disappeared beneath the water.

Mark had pulled out his phone to take a picture right before the object disappeared beneath the water's surface. He and Lisa stood there on the quiet beach, trying to grasp what they had seen. Mark checked the picture on his phone. It proved disappointingly small and slightly blurred. He put the phone back in his pocket.

Mark broke the silence. "Did we really see that, Lisa? It... it just disappeared!"

Lisa turned to Mark. "We saw what we saw, but you know nobody is going to believe us."

Mark insisted, "We need to report it, anyway," as he pulled his phone back out to dial.

***

At the sound of a knock on the door, Mark went to see who it could be.

"Hello, I'm Bill Williams from KBUZ Radio 103. Can I discuss what you saw on the beach last night?"

A reporter from the local radio station read the police reports and found the couple's report. The reporter got Mark's address from the police report.

Keeping the door partially closed, Mark answered, "There's not much to say. We saw a light, some ,,thing hovered over the water and then it went under."

The reporter persisted, "Could you guess how far away it appeared?"

Mark thought for a moment. "Probably about, I don't know, maybe half a mile out? It was hard to tell in the dark."

"Did you hear anything?"

"No, it didn't make any sound, at least not that we could hear over the waves."

Right then, Lisa peered around the door to see the conversation. "We told the police everything we saw. It appeared and disappeared. That's about it. It was there and then it wasn't. I told Mark nobody would believe us..."

"I'm afraid we don't have anything more to say. We would appreciate it if you wouldn't use our names in whatever you decide to report." The reporter nodded in agreement, turned and walked away as Mark closed the door.

"I wonder how many more times *that's* going to happen?" Lisa grimaced and walked back to the other room.

"Well, he handled it nicely" Mark went back to the couch and resumed reading something on his phone. "Hey Lisa, we weren't the only ones who saw that thing last night. It's all over social media. Some people are saying some pretty wild things about it. They're saying it shot a laser beam at an apartment building on the beach. I think it was only the lighthouse."

Lisa came back into the room. "That always seems to happen. People make up all kinds of stories. That's why I didn't want you to report it. It makes us look like the crazies."

***

Later that afternoon, the doorbell rang. Mark muttered something to himself as he went to the door. This time, it wasn't a reporter, though. Mark opened the door to see two men in dark suits, their features obscured by sunglasses and hats. Their pale complexion contrasted with the dark glasses. "Just like in the movies," Mark thought.

"We would like to speak with you about your 'encounter' last night," the first man said, holding out a white card with a strange logo and the word "Security" in the center. He didn't offer the card to Mark, but instead slipped it back into the inside pocket of his jacket. "May we come in?", not waiting for an answer, he said as he gently pressed against the door and moved inside. Lisa came around the corner from the hallway and the second man nodded toward her He. followed the first man into the room. The sunglasses remained on their faces.

As the men passed by, Lisa sensed a slight odor of ... something. Strange...

The two men did not offer to introduce themselves as the first one asked Mark, "We have some matters to discuss regarding your sighting last night." The man's face had no expression as he spoke.

Mark felt more than a little annoyed by the intrusion. "Do you mind telling me who you are?"

"You don't need to worry about that. We know who you are. Let's say we're from the government," he said. As he said it, the second man turned to face Lisa and briefly smiled. Lisa was now feeling even more uneasy.

"And what part of the government would that be?" Mark asked firmly.

"That doesn't matter," the man in black replied. "What were you doing on the beach last night?"

"We were out taking a walk," Mark said defensively.

"We have been monitoring reports of unusual phenomena in the area. Your report of a sighting caught our attention, and we are here to ensure the situation remains under control. What do you think you saw?" the second man asked.

Lisa interrupted, "I think you know what we saw…"

The second man spoke. "Your safety is our utmost priority. For that reason, we advise you to refrain from discussing this incident. Publicizing such events can lead to unnecessary panic and misinformation."

"But it's already on the radio and TV. There's even a group that formed on Facebook already…"

The first man broke in to say, "We're asking for your cooperation and understanding." There was an implied threat in the way he said it.

Lisa remained undaunted. "We have no reason to talk about it to anyone else. It's caused enough trouble already."

That seemed to satisfy the two strange men as they turned, opened the door for themselves, and left. Mark watched as they got into a dark car parked at the curb. As the car drove away, Mark tried to see the license plate, but he saw none and,; it the car disappeared into the traffic.

"Well, that was an experience," Mark said, looking to assess Lisa's reaction.

"Did you notice anything weird about those people, like their cologne? It just came to me, I swear, it was the smell of iodine. No, more like ammonia, I think."

"Now that you mention it…" Mark reached back to scratch the top of his head.

"I would like to know who those people were. Did you see anything, like a license tag, maybe?"

"I'm not sure if it even had a license tag. I couldn't see any," Mark said as he again checked his phone. "We're not the only ones who've had visitors. The people in that new Facebook group are talking about their visitors."

***

Lisa's skepticism grew stronger as the couple sat at the dining room table that evening. "I can't shake the feeling those two weren't who they said they were. Who can we talk to?" Lisa asked.

Mark checked Google and came up with an answer. "Maybe the Federal Aviation Administration and a few others."

"Do you expect the FAA to take us seriously?" Lisa said emphatically. Mark shook his head no in agreement.

"But I found this one organization," he said, pointing at his phone screen. "They have an online form. I say, let's fill it out and see what happens. It looks like we can upload the picture I took."

Lisa shrugged. "We're probably asking for more trouble."

***

Several days later, Mark's phone showed an incoming call from the website where he'd filed the report on their sighting. "Hello, this is Ben. I'm calling about your UFO report. Do you have a minute to talk?"

"Sure, but I don't want my personal information spread around," Mark said with concern.

"That concern may be why fewer than one in four hundred UAP or UFO sightings are reported. But about a quarter of the reports that we get have more than one witness. I can assure you that we are a full-time organization of professionals. We're only interested in the data, not your personal information. You gave a pretty good description of your experience online, and I see you uploaded a photo. Do you have any more information, and have you been back to that location since your experience that night?"

Mark switched on the phone speaker so that Lisa could hear and replied that they had not been back to the beach.

Ben continued. "We did get a few other reports, and one person said they saw the report on TV and went out to look. They said while they were watching, they saw an object come out of the water and streak away into the sky."

"Do you know anything about the two guys who came to visit us asking about what we saw?" Mark asked.

"I can't say. The government tells us they only respond when there are reports of physical evidence. So, somebody came to talk to you?"

Lisa answered the question. "Yes, two men showed up the next day. They asked questions, told us not to talk about it, and then left. They were really weird if you ask me."

"I have no answers for you. We have had reports of such visitors, but the government has told us they don't do that," Ben answered.

Mark and Lisa had nothing more to offer, so they thanked Ben for calling and said goodbye.

***

Mark remembered they had a video camera on the front door. He checked the video recording for the time the two men came to visit and rang the bell. As he scanned the video recording, he gasped. "Lisa, you were right. Come see this".

Lisa's eyes widened, her hand instinctively covering her mouth in disbelief. The sight before them appeared both mesmerizing and chilling, as the video showed the two agents with features that defied all human resemblance. Their eyes were large and almond-shaped, their skin had an otherworldly pallor, and their hands appeared elongated with slender fingers that ended in unnaturally sharp points.

"That's not how they looked to us", she exclaimed. "How did they do that? How did they make us see something totally different?"

Mark said softly, "I'm guessing they weren't government agents at all."

Lisa answered, "Ya think??!! That's scary. We were scared when we thought they were from the government, but now we're scared because maybe they might not be!"

Mark turned to Lisa. "This isn't at all what happens in the movies. Now we know why people don't like to talk about it when they see UFOs."

What Mark and Lisa saw in the doorbell camera video

If Dreams Could Speak

When paramedics arrived at the scene of the accident, they found Emily Foster unconscious and unresponsive. Her pulse registered weak, and her breathing appeared shallow. They loaded her onto a stretcher and rushed her to the hospital.

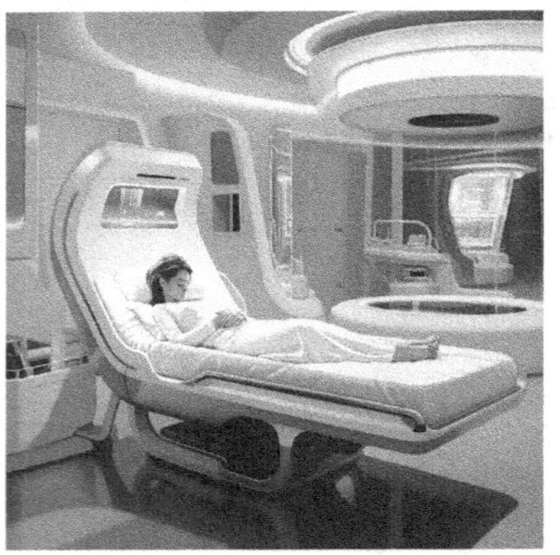

Moments before, Emily had been looking forward to a "girls' night out" with her sister, Rachel. Late in the afternoon, she approached an intersection. The light turned green, but she failed to notice the dark gray SUV fast approaching from the right. As the SUV collided with Emily's smaller car, it spun out and violently stopped at the curb.

The other driver suffered no serious injuries. She explained to the police that she had "blacked out" as she approached the intersection, possibly from her diabetic condition.

At the hospital, ER doctors examined Emily, but they could not find any apparent reason she remained unconscious. There were no visible indications of head trauma, so they began tests for other causes.

***

Rachel's eyes repeatedly flicked towards her phone screen as the minutes ticked away. The room grew dimmer with the advancing hour, and questions swirled in her mind about Emily's absence. A growing unease settled in her chest, tingling like a whisper of doubt. Then, as if to confirm her suspicions, the phone's buzz pierced the silence. She hesitated before answering, her heart racing, but the unfamiliar number on the caller ID only increased her fear.

"This is Officer Patterson from the police department. Are you Rachel Foster?" Rachel's heart sank as she answered with obvious concern, "Yes, I'm Rachel. Why are you calling?"

"I'm afraid I have some tough news about your sister, Emily. Your number was the emergency contact on the Lock Screen on her phone. There's been an accident, and they have transported her to the hospital."

"Is she alright?" Rachel asked.

"She doesn't appear to be seriously hurt, but you will need to come to the hospital. Emily is unconscious, and the doctors will want to ask you some questions."

As Rachel wiped away tears, she said, "OK, thank you. I'll be there as soon as I can". She would wait to call their mother until she knew more about Emily's condition.

***

The connection between the two sisters ran deep. Although separated by three years of age, they were otherwise like twins. Despite a three-year age gap, their bond went beyond finishing one another's sentences. Yet matching their schedules proved a perpetual challenge. Emily, a gifted graphic artist in the world of advertising, frequently devoted herself to laborious hours on specialized projects. At 29, Rachel's path had led her through nursing school to a bachelor's degree in nursing. But she had found her niche as an Occupational Health Nurse. Rachel's innate empathy set her apart, though it occasionally teetered on the brink of overwhelming compassion, prompting her to veer away from the relentless demands of hospital work. Her duties frequently entailed tending to accident victims and fostering a well-established partnership with the local hospital staff.

The wait seemed unbearable until Rachel heard her name called. A nurse beckoned her through heavy doors to a small room on the side of a large hallway. Dressed in pale blue scrubs, the duty nurse, Sarah Thompson, appeared to be older than Rachel, perhaps in her late thirties, with a kind expression and short curly brown hair.

"Hi, Rachel, you're Emily's sister, right?" the nurse asked.

"Yes, is she going to be OK?" Rachel answered, flicking a bit of her hair away from her eyes.

"We can't say for sure now. We ran a few tests and hope to have some answers soon. There weren't any signs of head injury, but the doctors ordered a CT scan and an MRI, just to be sure."

Rachel wanted to know, "When can I see her?"

"We'll call you when she is back from the tests."

***

Returning to a seat in the ER waiting room, Rachel resolved to break the news to their mom. She hesitated, her thoughts gathering the words she needed to say as she dialed the number.

"Hi, Mo," she said as her mom, Jennifer, answered. "I'm at the hospital, with Emily. There's been an accident, but Emily's OK. I didn't call right away until I found out more. I don't want you to worry too much."

Rachel discouraged her mom, Jennifer, from coming to the hospital, but, of course, her mom insisted on coming, anyway.

Later, as Jennifer arrived at the ER, she came and sat next to Rachel, holding her daughter's hand.

A middle-aged nurse took up her duty, her hair gathered in a neat bun.

Noticing the shift change at the nurse's station, Rachel went back to the desk to ask about any news.

"Excuse me," Rachel asked the new duty nurse, "Can you tell me if there's any news on my sister, Emily? "

"Of course," she said, "I'll check for you. What is your sister's name and date of birth?"

Rachel responded, "Emily Foster, May 12th, age 26."

"Thank you, let me see," as she typed the information into the computer. "It looks like they have transferred her to the ICU. I'll call up there and get an update on her condition for you."

"Thank you so much."

The nurse picked up the phone to call.

"Hi, this is the ER desk. Can you give me an update on Emily Foster? Her family is here, and they're worried about her."

Rachel overheard the ICU nurse on the phone. "They finished running the tests and took her back to her room." Rachel nodded in acknowledgment to the duty nurse and turned to repeat the information to her mother.

"Oh, thank goodness. Is she awake?" Jennifer asked.

The duty nurse relayed the question but shook her head no. "But you can go upstairs and wait there." She pointed to the doors on the left. "Go through those doors, and you'll find the elevators to the ICU on the fourth floor. The nurse's station can direct you to her room."

Rachel and her mom found the elevator, and on reaching the fourth floor, Rachel felt happy to see a familiar face. At the nurse's station, Susan Wells stood out with her curly red hair and bright blue eyes. Rachel knew her from nursing school. Susan appeared surprised and concerned to see Rachel. The two girls exchanged waves and smiles as Rachel approached the desk. Her mom sat in a chair in the hallway.

"I'm surprised to see you here. How are you?" the nurse asked.

Getting right to the point, Rachel said, "We're here to see my sister, Emily Foster. Can you tell us how to find her room?"

Susan glanced at the list on a clipboard. "She's in 410, but we can only let one of you visit at a time. She's still unconscious."

Rachel turned to her mom. "They only allow one at a time. You go first," and motioned to her to follow the nurse down the hall. After a few minutes, Jennifer and the nurse emerged from the room. Jennifer's face revealed the stress of concern. The nurse beckoned for Rachel.

Rachel turned to her mom. "Mom, it's late, and you should go home. I'll let you know if anything changes." Jennifer objected, but Rachel squeezed her mom's hand and smiled. "There's nothing you can do here. Better get some rest." Her mom nodded in agreement. The elevator door opened, and Jennifer looked back to see Rachel slipping into Emily's room.

The hospital room had a pleasant atmosphere, with off-white walls and a large window. The faint scent of disinfectant and medicine filled the air, accompanied by the steady beeping of the monitors.

Emily remained motionless in the center of the room, lying in a large hospital bed. White sheets and blankets covered her up to her chest. Medical equipment surrounded the bed, including a heart monitor screen, an oxygen tank, and an IV bag hanging from a stand. The monitors displayed graphs and numbers, tracking Emily's condition. The light from the monitors cast faint shadows on the walls.

After a few moments, Nurse Wells came to check on her patient. Rachel felt helpless as she stood next to her sister.

"Why is she still like this?" Rachel asks.

"Doctor Elliot said they don't know. She didn't suffer any serious injury; no broken bones, only some nasty bruises on her legs. They ran an MRI and some other tests, but you'll need to talk to the doctor for any more," the nurse explained.

Rachel felt worried. "But why?" she almost protested.

Nurse Wells told her, "I'm sorry, Rachel, I can't give you the answers about your sister's condition. However, I can tell you that the doctors will keep running tests until they find the reason."

"Are we sure she didn't hit her head in the accident?"

"I really can't tell you this, but they didn't find any sign of head trauma in the scans."

"Thank you. Can I stay with her for a while?" Rachel motioned toward the chair by the door. "I want to be with her."

"I don't think anybody will object. I'll check with Dr. Patel, the doctor on duty. If there's any problem, I'll let you know." The nurse pulled the door almost closed as she left.

Someone had recovered Emily's phone and purse from the wrecked car at the accident scene and thought to have them delivered it to the hospital.

Rachel found a small pillow in the room and tried to find a restful position in the chair as she gazed at Emily's face. In a short time, she drifted off to sleep. She dreamed about her sister, but the dream faded as Rachel stirred awake. She strained to see the dimly lit clock, showing something after two. As Saturday morning dawned, the hospital room door opened, and the duty doctor entered. He smiled at Rachel as he noted the readings on the medical monitors and Emily's charts.

"Good morning," he said. "I'll be taking care of your sister today."

"Thank you. Can you tell me anything?"

"We're still waiting for more test results, but the MRI and CT scans didn't show any brain damage or internal bleeding. However, we are checking for other conditions like stroke, aneurysm, or any other neurological issues. We're also checking for any underlying medical conditions that could have triggered the coma."

Rachel wanted to know, "What kind of conditions?"

"There are a few possibilities: a severe infection, metabolic abnormalities, or even a drug overdose. We're running some blood tests to check for those conditions as well."

Rachel stated adamantly, "Emily is not into drugs, I can assure you."

"I understand, but sometimes normal medications can have adverse reactions or interactions. We're checking for that possibility as well. Is there any family history of diabetes?"

"No, nothing like that. When will she wake up?" Rachel almost pleaded.

"It's hard to say at this point. We're doing everything we can to find the cause and decide on a treatment. But it's important to remember that recovery from a coma can be a slow and unpredictable process. We'll keep the family updated as we learn more." The doctor finished up, making some notes on the chart attached to Emily's bed as he left the room.

Rachel played a voicemail from her sister earlier in the day, perhaps to hear her voice. She reached out to touch Emily's hand. The beeping of the monitors had a hypnotic effect. Her hand fell as she again drifted off to sleep.

Again, she dreamed she saw her sister, but this time, Emily seemed she wanted to say something but couldn't. Strangely, Rachel sensed being thirsty.

Later, Susan Wells stopped by the room to check on the two girls. The sound of the heavy door awakened Rachel. She smiled to see Susan, hoping she could tell her about the dream.

"I had the strangest feeling," she told Susan. "You're going to think I'm crazy, but I saw Emily in a dream, and I felt like she wanted to tell me she's tired and very thirsty. Does that make any sense?"

"That really can't be," Susan answered. "The IV shows she's getting plenty of fluid. We keep track of that on her charts."

Dr. Elliot came in to check on Emily. The doctor, in his early 40s, had short black hair, almost like a military cut, with slight touches of gray. "Do we know who her doctor is?" he asked.

Rachael thought for a moment and then shook her head. "She told me she changed doctors a while back, but I'm sorry. I don't remember who her new doctor is."

Doctor Elliot thought for a moment. "It could be another dead end, but I would like to know if she's reacting to something prescribed."

Nurse Wells looked toward Rachel and then to the doctor as she asked, "Is it crazy to think that the patient might try to reach out to her sister in her dreams?"

Dr. Elliot looked surprised, but then he smiled. "A coma is a state of profound unconsciousness in which a person cannot be awakened and does not respond to stimuli. There is no clear scientific evidence to support the idea that a person in a coma can communicate through dreams. While people in a coma may exhibit some brain activity and may even experience dreams, there is currently no reliable way to communicate with them. I'm sorry."

Susan turned to Rachel, "This is the end of my shift, and the hospital has a great cafeteria, and they should be open about now. Maybe we can talk over breakfast?" Disappointed by the doctor's response, Rachel nodded in agreement, and they walked to the elevators.

The hospital cafeteria bustled with activity as the two girls joined the line. They worked their way through the food selections and found an open table.

As they sat down, Susan asked, "Tell me about your dream."

"It felt so real! It was like she knew I was there, and she was trying to reach out to me for help. She didn't say anything, but I had the sensation of being trapped. And thirsty. All I can think of is that was experiencing what Emily was feeling. I bet Dr. Elliot thinks I'm crazy. I bet he thinks we're *both* crazy."

"Maybe." Susan stretched her neck to see someone behind Rachel. "But I think I see someone who can help. Excuse me for a minute." She stood and walked over to where an older gentleman dressed in a suit was emptying his tray in the container. She spoke with him briefly, and followed her back to their table.

"This is Dr. Eugene Phelps. He's a neurologist who stops by occasionally as a consultant. I told him about your dreams, and he might have some different ideas."

Dr. Phelps pulled up a chair from an empty table nearby. "Hi, Rachel, I understand you experienced something in a dream. Tell me about it."

Rachel felt relieved. "I dreamed I saw her calling out to me, but she said nothing. I had a feeling of being trapped. It felt like Emily knew what had happened, and she tried to tell me..." Her voice trailed off as she gestured upward with her hands.

The doctor pursed his lips and tilted his head a bit before he spoke. "Tell me about how all this started. Why is your sister here?"

Rachel and the nurse pieced together the story of the past twenty-four hours for Dr. Phelps: the accident, the coma, the testing.

They explained the doctors didn't understand why Emily remained unconscious.

"I see. Interesting," Dr. Phelps said. "I'm not going to tell you that you're crazy. Not at all. There's a history of research in this area that even goes back to Nikola Tesla and the 1880s. I recently saw a study by Dr. Stanley Critur at Saybrook University in California, citing a wealth of material supporting the possibility of telepathic effects occurring during dreams. There are several books on the subject. Let me speak with your doctor. We may have uncovered a clue."

Rachel felt relieved and thanked the doctor as they finished their breakfast.

***

Rachel needed to go home and change, but she couldn't leave. She returned to Emily's room. Emily remained the same, still unconscious. The door to the room stood open, and Rachel glanced down the hall to see Dr. Phelps talking with Dr. Elliot, who had arrived on shift. Soon, both doctors walked toward Emily's room. They acknowledged Rachel but didn't speak. Dr. Elliot handed Emily's chart to Dr. Phelps and studied his response. Dr. Phelps nodded. Rachel smiled hopefully as her eyes followed the two doctors as they left the room.

Not long after, Dr. Elliot returned to the room. "Dr. Phelps thinks we may have overlooked something. We're going to run a different test on Emily. That might solve the puzzle for us." He reached out and grasped Rachel's hand. "Don't give up! Maybe you can wait outside while we set up."

Rachel reluctantly left the room to wait down the hallway as two nurses entered. A few moments later, one nurse left and returned with a blood glucose meter. About an hour had elapsed when Rachel finally saw Dr. Elliot coming toward her.

"I think we found the secret. In my consultation with Dr. Phelps, we looked more closely at your sister's bloodwork. On his suggestion, we found a case study describing a similar presentation of acute adrenal crisis in a minor trauma patient."

The doctor explained, "The adrenal glands produce vital hormones, including cortisol and aldosterone. In Emily's case, they failed to function properly, possibly because of the shock of the accident. Her body could not produce sufficient amounts of the hormones, which led to her condition. We tried an emergency intravenous steroid infusion to replace the lack of cortisol. She seemed to respond positively. I can't explain how, but the message about her being thirsty was the clue we needed."

The doctor continued, "In Emily's case, the shock from the accident likely caused a disruption in her adrenal gland function. Without adequate cortisol production, her body couldn't respond appropriately to stress, leading to a range of symptoms. One of the key indicators we noticed was her excessive thirst. This showed that her adrenal glands were not functioning properly, as the imbalance in electrolytes caused by inadequate aldosterone production can lead to increased thirst."

***

Hours later, Rachel watched as Emily stirred, her eyes fluttering open. As her vision adjusted to the soft light of the room, she turned her head to see Rachel standing by her side with a look of sheer relief and joy. Without hesitation, Rachel reached for the call button, pressing it urgently. Within moments, a nurse entered the room, the sound of her footsteps echoing against the tiled floor.

"Emily is awake!" Rachel exclaimed, her voice filled with a mix of excitement and anticipation.

The day nurse smiled warmly at the sight of Emily's conscious gaze. "Oh, thank goodness! I'll inform Dr. Elliot right away," she said, reaching for the phone to notify the doctor of Emily's awakening.

Emily awakened. "Rachel... Rachel, is that you?" "

"Welcome back! How are you feeling?"

Emily's mind swirled with confusion. She turned to her sister and said, "I had the strangest dream. I remember seeing you. I tried to tell you..."

Rachel smiled. "I know. You were in my dream, and you told me you felt thirsty. The doctors didn't know what to do. I told them about my dream, but it was hard to make them believe me."

"Is that possible? ...that you heard me? Wow, I can't wrap my head around it. It's amazing to think that we could connect that way."

Rachel reached out to hold her sister's hand. "I know. It's hard to believe. The doctors couldn't figure out how to help you, but when you told me about being thirsty in your dream, that was the clue. That's how the doctors brought you back."

"You were always there for me, big sister. I really can't wrap my head around all this, but I'm sure glad we have each other."

"That's all that counts, right, Em?"

Dr. Elliot arrived. His eyes lit up with delight as he saw Emily. He walked over to her bedside, checked the monitors, and confirmed that her vital signs were stable. Dr. Elliot stepped closer and stood beside Rachel. "Emily, it's wonderful to see you awake. How are you feeling?"

Emily's lips curved into a weak but grateful smile. "I... I'm glad to be back, that's for sure!" she said, her voice barely above a whisper as the emotion of the moment took over her.

Rachel's eyes welled up with tears as she took Emily's hand in her own. "Oh, Em, you do not know how relieved I am. I knew you were in there all along."

Dr. Elliot leaned in closer, his eyes focused on Emily's face, attentive to every word and expression. "Emily, we're so glad you've come back to us," he said, his voice filled with sincerity. "During your coma, we discovered you were experiencing locked-in syndrome, a condition where you were conscious but unable to move or communicate. It had been a difficult situation to diagnose initially, but thanks to Rachel's, hmmm, clue, we found the underlying cause."

Emily's eyes widen with curiosity and a renewed sense of hope. "What caused it, doctor? And what do we need to do to correct it?"

Dr. Elliot took a deep breath, his gaze conveying a mixture of compassion and professionalism. Answering the unspoken question on Emily's face, he said, "It appears that you had an unusual electrolyte imbalance that affected your nervous system, causing the locked-in syndrome. You were in an accident and something about that shock set it off. We'll need to keep a close eye on your electrolyte levels and provide targeted treatment to restore the balance. With time and proper care, we believe you can make a full recovery."

The weight of Emily's condition lifted, replaced by a renewed sense of hope and determination. She looked at Rachel, their eyes meeting with an unspoken understanding of their journey together.

Emily said, "Let's do whatever it takes. I'm ready to go home!"

Dr. Elliot nodded, his gaze reflecting admiration for Emily's resilience. "Emily. I'll ensure you receive the best care possible, and we'll work towards restoring your health and independence."

Somebody had brought Emily's phone from the accident scene and delivered it to the hospital. Emily noticed it on the bedtable and used it to leave a voicemail message for her boss, explaining her absence.

Over the next few days, Emily underwent a series of tests and treatments to address the electrolyte imbalance. Dr. Elliot and his medical team monitored her progress, setting the medications and fluids to restore balance and support her recovery.

Rachel asked for more time off from her job to stay with Emily..

Early one morning, Emily sat up in her hospital room as daylight peeked through the window. Dr. Elliot came in with a smile on his face.

"Good morning! Emily, your tests show significant improvement," Dr. Elliot announced confidently. "Your electrolyte imbalance is back to normal. I think you're about ready to go home. Your sister is already on the way."

Emily's eyes sparkled with hope and relief. The nurse assistant rolled her out to the hospital entrance. As Rachel helped her sister into her car, she asked, "So, what again are we going to do for our girls' night out?"

Emily thought for a moment and said, "No, let's go see mom. We can go to the movies any time."

A smile played across Rachel's lips as she nodded in agreement. "You're right, Em. Let's go see mom. She's been waiting for this moment as eagerly as we have," she said as she started the engine.

As they drove, the streetlights cast ethereal shadows on the pavement. The cool breeze whispered through the open windows.

As they arrived, the early dawn bathed their childhood home in a warm glow. Rachel pulled into the driveway, and the sisters stepped to the front door. Their mom had been waiting and heard the car as they drove up. The door opened, and Rachel raised her hand to knock. The reunion was filled with emotion. As the girls came inside, the three of them formed a circle of love and support. The worries, the pain, and the uncertainty of the past days seemed to melt away in that moment, replaced by a renewed sense of hope and gratitude.

With tears of joy streaming down her cheeks, Jennifer marveled at her daughter's strength and resilience. "You two share an un-breakable bond, a connection that goes beyond the physical. I've always believed that the love between sisters is unique, but you've truly opened my eyes to its incredible power."

Rachel gazed out the window at the new day, marveling at the magic of dreams and the connection between them. Her sister's miraculous return stood as a testament to the incredible power of the human spirit and the special love shared between sisters.

The Company Hired a Robot

B eep – Beep – Beep – Beep!

Shipping and receiving manager David Lee looked up from paperwork on his desk through the window of his small office as a delivery truck backed up to the loading dock. He recognized the name of the local delivery company. He punched the button on his phone to call the Information Technology manager's office. Tomi Singh answered, "What's up, David?"

"Your new toy is here." David punched the button to disconnect the call without waiting for a response.

Dave Lee had been with the company for more than ten years. He took pride in keeping the shipping and receiving area organized and efficient. His stern approach doesn't fool anyone. He's well-liked by the people who work at the company. He also doesn't like to waste time on formalities. As he walked out onto the loading dock, the driver opened the squeaky roll-up door of the delivery van and handed him a clipboard. Inside the truck stood a single large crate with big black letters that spelled out "Robotic Office System for Communication and Operational Efficiency." David signed the delivery order and handed it back to the driver.

Tomi soon arrived as David rolled the large pallet jack under the crate in the delivery van to move it onto the loading dock.

In his early thirties, Tomi Singh always kept up with the latest technology trends. Dedicated to finding innovative solutions to IT problems, this was Tomi's new baby. He convinced the board of directors and the CEO, Robert Johnson, that an artificial intelligence mobile robot could improve the company's efficiency and productivity. Johnson interpreted that in dollar signs.

As the news spread, more people arrived at the loading dock. The shipment excited some employees, but not so much for others, like HR director Robert Jones. Bob was among the doubters. He expressed concern about how employees might react to this machine's intrusion.

Last to arrive was Emily Jones, the Tech Support specialist. In her early twenties, she was naturally a problem-solver, open to new things if they would help her clients. She welcomed the new arrival to help her better manage technical support.

Someone in the group located a flatbed dolly. The crate was loaded on, and the people who had gathered on the loading dock filtered back to their offices. David and his assistant, Alex, rolled the crate to the freight elevator and up to the IT office. Inside the crate were several parts wrapped in plastic, along with bundled cables, motors, and other components. Tomi moved closer to inspect. As his hand rubbed the back of his head, he muttered, "Some assembly required." Alex picked out one of the heavier boxes and proclaimed: "Yes, but the battery *is included!*" As the various parts came together, ROSCOE took a familiar robotic shape. It had mechanical rollers, a display screen, and a robot head, complete with camera sensors for the eyes, while a pattern of holes covered a speaker where a mouth should be. There were sensor units at every point. The articulated arms included gripper-hands with connectors for various motorized tools and utility attachments. A small panel of connectors decorated the back panel above the battery compartment.

Tomi had been reading the manual and reviewing online videos, so he knew exactly what to do. As he connected the last of the modules, he lifted the battery into place. The fiber optic cable connected the LAN (Local Area Network) port to the company's mainframe rack. IT assistant Alex looked on as Tomi pressed the control switch before he closed and latched the battery panel. The machine responded with a hum and a whir of motors as it came to life, concluding with a beep. The readout on the front panel screen spelled out the initials "R.O.S.C.O.E" and the word "Ready!" At a nearby terminal, Tomi logged into the robot's admin interface and replaced the default with a secure password. Next, he went about configuring the robot's access to the company's Wi-Fi network so it could operate freely about the building. And of course, the robot could speak. Alex and Tomi browsed the selection until they decided on an appropriate voice for "ROSCOE". The voice they chose sounded dignified but not stuffy, somewhat smooth and almost melodic. The voice might allow employees to feel comfortable responding to a machine. At least, as comfortable as they could be, to a five-foot-tall metal and plastic box moving around on tread rollers.

On command, the internal artificial intelligence engine went about accumulating data. As it scanned in the data, the data screen displayed the company's department directories and documents, including employee photos, mapping out various locations within the building. The robot's optical sensors would enable it to navigate the hallways and recognize employees. This was the part that had Tomi worried. He had no serious concerns about data security. Security functions were built into the system framework. The manufacturer had satisfied those concerns for Tomi. What he was more concerned about was the reaction of the staff as they came to realize how much information the robot had stored.

What was more impressive was that the machine, the artificial intelligence that allowed it to gain new knowledge as it gained more and more input data. It could analyze information and suggest improvements in marketing documents and accounting spreadsheets. ROSCOE could even access phone system data and manage traffic levels at various times.

Finally, the time came to introduce ROSCOE to the board of directors and the CEO. CEO Johnson was a seasoned business-executive type who appeared to be in his early fifties. He presented an image of a leader expecting a high level of performance. Not so much ambitious as he was focused on growing the company. Tomi and Alex had convinced him that ROSCOE would help him achieve his goals. The board members, elected by the stockholders seated at the long executive table, showed no sign of doubting the decision. Actually, the board members rarely displayed any expressions at all.

Well, there was one. That *one* was Jack Thompson. He hid a smirk as the trio from IT entered the boardroom. Jack had always been skeptical of new technology and Artificial Intelligence in particular. As Jack caught Tomi's eye, the smirk became a forced smile.

While the CEO looked on from one end of the table, Tomi, and Alex stood at the other and described ROSCOE's capabilities and advantages for the board. Nex it came time for ROSCOE to take over. ROSCO took control of the presentation on the large screen at the end of the large boardroom. The presentation listed the advantages of the new mobile artificial intelligence robot technology. The board appeared impressed and the CEO smiled his approval as Alex issued a voice command to ROSCOE. The trio left the room together.

The CEO and the board members voiced no objections, which meant that ROSCOE had passed the first test.

The corporate website created a central hub for employees to access important information and communicate. It helped them to carry out their daily tasks even when working from home or off-site. As the first task, ROSCOE generated a scheduling system. The system provided a way for employees to schedule a visit from the robot. The robot accessed the internal Content Management System and began constructing a new welcome screen. It detailed how to use the new resources and included illustrated examples. Next, ROSCOE accessed the network database and generated a calendar that was connected to the corporate scheduling system. ROSCOE created an internal email message sent to each employee.

Job completed, ROSCOE announced, "Ready," as the robot's front panel screen spelled out the word at the same time.

***

First to sign up for ROSCO's aid, Emily headed the company's Technical Support team. She expressed the need to streamline the system to make it easier for customers to get the answers.

ROSCOE rolled into her office, stopped in front of her desk, and greeted her by name. A bit surprised to hear the robot speaking directly to her, Emily ran through a prepared list of problems she needed to solve.

Emily asked ROSCOE, "How can we handle surges of customer online contacts that sometimes overwhelm our limited staff?"

ROSCOE's voice responded, "Instead of your current text window, we propose a new chatbot powered by Artificial Intelligence. We'll program it to identify the most common problems and use the customer files to provide answers."

"The AI can gather the customer's information and generate an accurate response to their questions in real-time," said ROSCOE.

Emily was concerned. "What about my staff?"

"The system can handle many customer contacts at once, eliminating hold-time and routing only the more complex questions to your staff. If a customer's question requires human help, the system can seamlessly hand off the conversation to your support staff, along with providing all the relevant information and context to ensure a smooth transition.".

"How long will it take to create that system?" Emily asked.

Generating computer programming is something Artificial Intelligence is especially good at doing. ROSCOE linked the new chatbot response system to the company's customer database and logins. In a short time, ROSCOE's screen spelled out the now familiar "READY" response as ROSCOE announced: "Let's test it".

Emily created a test customer login and account information. She logged into the company's website from her phone. She paused for a moment and typed in a complex question. The new chatbot responded with a link to an appropriate resource to answer the question.

"But what if it can't find the right answer?" Emily asked. "Most of the complaints are about the time to get answers."

ROSCOE said, "Ask an impossible question."

Emily knew what to do. She typed in a question with confusing wording based on a tough call they had recently handled. The chatbot analyzed the message and apologized to the customer for not having an appropriate answer. It asked the customer to wait for a human response while it switched the customer to the support staff. The complete text conversation was delivered to the support staff member's screen, along with a summary of the customer's contact and product information. Randy, the support tech, saw that he had all the information to work from and responded to the "test" customer on the chat screen.

Impressed by the result, Emily continued, "We have one native Spanish speaker on staff. Can we include a Spanish option, and if a human response is needed, can that customer be directed to our Spanish speaker?"

"That program module is activated. Spanish customers can only connect with the right staff person," ROSCOE responded.

"But what about voice calls?"

Once again, ROSCOE had a ready answer. "We will integrate voice recognition software into the system in the same way. It will answer in a human voice and offer an alternate language option. It will respond the same as the chatbot. The system will learn from the questions asked and build the data resource. If it can't provide a suitable answer, it will route the call to your support staff. That way, your staff can manage a larger number of calls with minimal hold time." ROSCOE promised to have the software generated and integrated into the phone system for testing the next day.

"It feels strange thanking a computer...." Emily said.

ROSCOE made a beep sound, then turned and left the room.

The next request came from Sarah Rodriguez in Marketing. A natural communicator in her early thirties, Sarah had a good understanding of marketing. Most important, a good listener, she took time to understand the other person's perspective. Active on social media, she kept up with the pulse of her market community.

ROSCOE rolled into Sarah's office at the exact time of the scheduled appointment. Sarah, however, had concerns about how her staff would react to a robot. She began with a simple task: "Hello, ROSCOE. We need to find the right target audience for our new product line. Can you do that?"

ROSCOE said, "Let us connect to your terminal so you can direct me to the product line."

Sarah brought up the file for the new product line.

ROSCOE scanned the document files and images and began generating text output: "Here's a list of our current customers who might be interested in the new products. We will generate a newsletter for your review, and you can send it to those customers. I'll also create some sample social media posts. You'll find the files in a special folder on your home screen."

Sarah smiled. "That would have taken me a long time. I'm sure glad to have you around!"

Nearby, Luke Elliot, the staff artist, felt his job threatened by AI-generated graphics. He even made doodles on his notepad, showing a robot melting into a blob on the floor. However, of course, he made sure his boss, Sarah, didn't see those drawings.

Next came John Stephens in Human Resources. At the scheduled time, ROSCOE rolled down the hall and came to a stop in front of John's desk.

Robert got right to the point: "I need a simple way to evaluate employee job performance for the quarter."

ROSCOE responded: "We can generate a report with all the relevant data. Would you like me to send it to your company email?"

"That would be good. When can you get it to me?" Robert asked.

"Check your email now. Is there anything we missed?" ROSCOE replied.

"I'll look it over and let you know. Can I reply to your email?"

"Yes. You may respond to the email." ROSCOE answered. "What else do you need to be more effective in your job?"

Robert nodded toward the staff as he described his next concern. "We have a lot of employees. The turnover is not excessive, but I'm concerned about potential threats from former employees. We need a defense strategy to prevent unauthorized access to the building. What can we do?"

Again, ROSCOE had a solution. "We have accessed the photo ID files of all current and former employees. We can integrate facial recognition into the security cameras to prevent unauthorized access to the building. We can compile a cost/benefit report for approval by the accounting department.

Robert responded sternly, "Most mass shootings take place at the workplace. That could address my most serious concerns."

The robot beeped, and the screen blinked "READY" as ROSCOE moved to the hallway and back to the IT department for the next task.

Lisa Martinez, in the Facilities Management office, had only glanced at the notices about updating passwords when she found an email in her inbox telling her that her password had expired, and she assumed a connection.

Subject: Password Expiration Notice:

Hello Lisa,

I hope this message finds you well. I am reaching out to let you know that your company password is set to expire soon. In order to ensure the security of our system, we require all users to renew their passwords on a regular basis.
Please follow the link to access the password reset page:
CLICK HERE
Once there, you will be able to create a new password that meets our new security requirements.
If you have any issues with this process or have any

questions, please don't hesitate to contact me.

Best regards,
Information Technology Department

When Lisa clicked *HERE*, it brought up what appeared to be the regular company login screen. Lisa did not think to notice the different URL in the browser address bar. She entered her password, and a message on the screen thanked her for "renewing" her password. She wondered why she had not been required to make a new password, but thought nothing of it.

Within minutes, a hacker used Lisa's password to log into the company's network and got to work exploring exposed documents and files on Lisa's terminal. At that exact moment, ROSCOE detected the login from an unauthorized external internet address or IP. A quick check of an online resource revealed it originated from a local internet service provider. ROSCOE promptly isolated Lisa's computer from the network, limiting the damage to the files on her computer. The hacker had briefly gained access to the company server, but the most sensitive data remained still secured behind a security firewall.

Meanwhile, ROSCOE alerted Tomi, who blocked the intruder's access by resetting Lisa's password. He ran a scan of the entire network to make sure there were no new hidden files. He reported the steps to ROSCOE through an isolated side network. ROSCOE began a deep scan of the system for any malware that might have been installed. Lisa's computer would also need to be carefully scanned for hidden "bots" that might have been set for later activation.

ROSCOE reviewed Lisa's email account and discovered the fake email notice. ROSCOE next posted a notice on the company forum warning against realistic-looking fake email notices about password expirations and communicated the information about the hacker's source IP address to Tomi. Tomi conferenced with the CEO, along with Tom Watson, in the legal department, as they agreed to contact local law enforcement.

***

A short time later, two investigators arrived at the front reception desk. One detective, Lt. Brown. The other officer's badge identified him as Sgt. Jones. They asked to be escorted to Tomi's office on the second floor. When they arrived at the IT office, they saw ROSCOE tethered to the network servers by a fiber-optic cable.

The officers were not expecting to see a robot. Sgt. Jones asked Tomi, "What's THAT thing?".

Tomi replied, "That's ROSCOE, our mobile AI system. It detected the intrusion and blocked off the affected terminal from the network. Lt. Brown smiled with an understanding nod. Brown mentioned to Tomi he had been qualified in cyber security. Tomi explained how the hacker had gained access through a compromised employee password. The officers asked what they knew about the extent of damage, potential motives, and recent employee terminations.

Tomi responded, "Yes, we have had a few employees leave, but I don't recall any who left under bad circumstances."

Lt. Brown asked, "Can you provide us with a list of those employees?" Tomi nodded yes.

"We traced the intrusion to this IP address. We traced it to a local Internet provider, so the intruder is not far away." Tomi said, handing Officer Brown a section of a log printout with the intruder's information.

The other officer asked, "Is there any other information that you think might be pertinent to this situation?"

Alex stood nearby, listening to the conversation, and looked puzzled as he looked at Tomi.

Tomi turned toward Alex, "He means, do we have any suspicions?" Turning to the officer, he said, "We'll let you know if we come up with anything."

After the officers' departure, Tomi called Lisa's extension. She sounded upset and worried, explaining that her computer began acting strangely. Tomi assured her he and Alex would visit her office to address the issue. Lisa's response sounded relieved. Her computer had been isolated from the main network, so she had not seen the notice warning about not responding to fake password reset notices via email.

Tomi and Alex arrived to find Lisa still stressed and bewildered about the situation. She described how her computer seemed to be haunted, with the cursor moving by itself until it stopped. After that, she couldn't do anything. The computer refused to work.

Tomi began, "Tell me about the email, the one about your password."

"It said it was from you. It said I had to renew my password. I think I saw something about that on the company forum, but I didn't pay much attention. A little later, my computer went crazy...." Lisa looked perplexed.

"I did not send that email," Tomi explained. "A fake tricked you. But we're lucky we have ROSCOE. The robot detected a hacker in your computer and isolated it to prevent the damage from spreading. We need to scan your computer to make sure nothing nasty got planted inside. That will take some time. Alex brought you a laptop so you can get back to work. It already has you logged in with a temporary password. You can take it to the other desk while Alex gets to work on your computer. Don't worry. No serious damage occurred, and the police are investigating. You need to be more cautious. And read the notices on the company forum more carefully, ok?" He smiled at Lisa. She relaxed a bit and smiled back as she accepted the laptop and took it to a nearby desk.

Meanwhile, Alex ran the scanning software on Lisa's computer. "Nothing so far," he told Tomi. "Maybe they only copied some files."

***

Alarm bells rang in the security office. The new facial recognition system had detected an unauthorized person at the employee entrance. Marcus, the chief of security, checked the camera. A pass lock keypad and a camera secured the interior door. He sees a hooded person using a metal rod to strike the break-proof glass on the inside employee entrance door. There was no one else in the room, so he pressed a button that locked the outer door, trapping the dangerous intruder inside. That also prevented any employees from entering the enclosed entrance. Pressing an intercom button, he instructed the intruder to remain calm and await the police. Next, he called 9-1-1 and reported an unauthorized intruder had been trapped in the employee entryway. The operator told him officers were on the way. By then, the security camera software had identified the intruder as a former employee.

Marcus Johnson had once been a military officer. Now, in his second career, he still looked the part, with a muscular build and closely shaved hair. He was comfortable with new technology, but he admitted he still had reservations about ROSCOE. That might change.

Twenty minutes later, his extension rang, and he let the officers in. They took the unauthorized intruder into custody without a struggle and transported him to the police station for interrogation. If the company pressed charges, the initial offense could be trespassing or unauthorized entry.

But so far, the motive remains a mystery. Tomi made a copy of the security video and sent it to the police to include in their investigation. The facial recognition system did not identify the intruder as a former employee.

The police interrogation of the intruder did not provide any useful information until they ran a fingerprint check. They confirm the identity of twenty-seven-year-old Michael Williams. His only previous conviction was related to theft at a warehouse where he had been employed. Williams refused to provide any motivation for attempting to access the building. A common thug would have tried to smash the keypad, but he had attacked the security glass on the door instead. The police were holding Williams, awaiting word from the company attorney. The attorney would let them know if the company would press charges for the damage. A final decision on that needed to come from the CEO. The company provided a summary of William's brief time as an employee.

Meanwhile, ROSCOE reviewed the computer access log for the employee entrance passkey. Tomi had taken the precaution of changing her access code when her company password was updated. During the intrusion, the access log recorded several attempts using Lisa's employee passcode key. ROSCOE passed that information to. Tomi and Alex immediately related it to the hacker's attack on Lisa's computer. Break-ins don't fit the profile of the average hacker. What was the connection?

The investigating officers brought in the two officers who had responded to the hacking complaint. Detective Lt. Brown and another officer arrived at the CEO's office at nine the next morning. As they sat down, Robert Johnson asked, "What have you come up with?"

Brown began, "The officers who worked on your intruder incident had reason to suspect a connection to the hacking event you called us about. It turns out they were right. We identified the location where the hacker sent the fake email. Your robot's information identified the entry code the intruder tried to use unsuccessfully. The suspect is in custody, awaiting a hearing on the attempted breaking and entering charge. We intend to add computer crime charges stemming from the hacker attack on your employee."

Johnson smiled, "Well, that's good news!"

"Yes, but there's some bad news," Brown continued. "We needed to find the motive. We kept pressing the prisoner until he finally admitted he got paid to make you look bad. The transaction took place in cash from an unknown party he met at a local bar. We have a video from the bar, but Williams was the only one we could identify. From what we can tell, it appears the intruder intended to make it look like you wasted the company's money on the new mobile computer robot. Can you think of anyone who would be motivated to do that?"

The CEO's face looked serious for a moment as he tried to decide how to respond. Someone might want to do that, but would that be enough to accuse the police?

He began, "I might, but if I'm mistaken, it could create serious problems. Can we keep this confidential?"

The officers agreed. "Who do you suspect?" the second officer asked.

"This can't get out," jotting a name on a notepad along with some other information. He didn't want anyone nearby to hear him say it out loud.

The officers looked at the notepad. "Do you have a photo?"

The CEO nodded and pulled a photo from a file folder in the horizontal file cabinet behind his desk.

Later that day, the detectives returned to the bar where Michael Williams said he had met with the stranger who hired him. The bar owner directed them to the bartender. The officers showed the bartender the picture they got from the CEO, and he remembered seeing the man in the picture. He had stood out because he didn't fit in with the usual customers at the bar.

Officer Johnson spotted the security camera above the cash register and went to the owner's office to ask to view the video recordings. The owner said they stored the recordings off-site, but she would ask the security company to make a copy for the police.

After a few days, the security company delivered the video files on a data drive to the police station. Detective Lt. Brown sifted through the video and found Williams, the man they had in custody, standing with Jack Thompson. That provided the connection they needed and enough suspicion to bring the board member in for questioning.

***

Jack Thompson, a prominent and wealthy individual, described himself as an investor and entrepreneur. His address was, not surprisingly, in a gated subdivision. The officer and the detective presented their identification at the gate. They found the address and walked up to the front door. Brown looked up at the security camera as he pressed the button. After a moment, as the detective raised his hand to knock, the door opened. Thompson had a scowl on his face.

"I'm Detective Lt. George Brown, and this is my partner, Sergeant Steve Jones. We need to talk to you about the recent attack at the company where you serve on the board of directors."

Thompson stiffened as he stepped back into the doorway. "I know nothing about it."

Sergeant Jones asked, "Are you sure? We have reason to believe you know the intruder who attempted to get past the entrance security."

Thompson shook his head. "I come in contact with a lot of people," he insisted.

"Mr. Thompson, we need you to come to the station to discuss it. You can give us your side of the story there."

Thompson stood firm. "I'm not going anywhere with you. You don't have any evidence."

"I'm afraid we do. We have a confession from the man you hired," said Sergeant Jones.

After a brief hesitation, Thompson sighed and shrugged. "Fine!" he said. "Let me grab my coat."

***

The CEO, called a special board meeting for Monday morning at 9 am. The notice only said there would be information about the recent security incidents.

The board members gathered, and the CEO introduced the two officers. Detective Brown spoke first.

"As you may know, we have been investigating the cyberattack, and the attempted break-in. Through our investigation, and with the help of your IT department, we connected the events, resulting in two arrests. The first arrest is Michael Williams, an individual who was hired to hack into your network. He was also the person who had been trapped at the employee entrance. We remain unsure of his intentions, had he successfully gained access through the employee entrance. He is known to hold grudges against large companies, possibly stemming from his release from his employment at a local warehouse."

One of the board members spoke up. "You said there were two arrests?"

"That's correct," said Officer Jones. "The other person is a member of this board." A gasp filled the room as the board members looked around.

Jones continued, "You may have noticed the absence of Mr. Jack Thompson. We took him into custody late yesterday, and he has been released on bond pending trial. According to the confession we obtained from Mr. Williams, Thompson paid him to make your CEO look bad in front of his board members. It appears Mr. Thompson resented Mr. Johnson's selection as CEO. A judge approved our request for a search warrant, and we got more evidence from Mr. Thompson's residence. We believe we have enough for the District Attorney to charge him with conspiracy to commit cybercrime and possibly as an accomplice to the attempted break-in.

Detective Brown was next to speak. "We need to acknowledge the special help that was provided in solving this case. We were assisted by two individuals in your Information Technology office and one more. That would be our new mechanical friend, Mr. ROSCOE.

The board responded with polite applause directed to the two officers and to ROSCOE. The officers turned to leave but not before giving a short wave of salute at ROSCOE.

Board member Susan Worth leaned over to Mary Wiggins: "I knew this robot would be a good thing".

Mary glanced over at ROSCOE and turned back to Susan as she whispered, "You're not going to believe this, but I think that darn robot winked at me!"

Interview with an Alien

In Nexus Broadcasting Network's dimly lit satellite control room, racks of equipment hummed with the soft whir of computer fans. Mark Foster, the network satellite engineer, sat at his control monitor. He glanced at the clock above the door as he awaited a scheduled feed from the West Coast. Startled by a sound, he looked up at the satellite feed monitor to see a strange creature. Mark shivered as his mind flashed back to a past experience as he fixed his stare on the screen.

Jolted back to his senses by the call buzzer on the IFB intercom, he pressed the talk button and said quickly, did not see "Let me get back to you."

"We have a problem with the feed," came the reply from the West Coast satellite truck.

"Yes, I know," Replied Mark. I'll get back to you." Obviously, they did not see what he was seeing.

The alien creature on the screen began speaking with a strange accent, reminiscent of robot voices in the movies or artificial intelligence voice generators. Mark instinctively reached to press the feed record function on his console.

"I am Zypteron," it said. The alien creature had large, almond-shaped eyes set in an overly large gray head devoid of visible ears. The alien's head had no hair and tapered past a tiny nose to a small mouth that did not move when it spoke. Its pale gray skin was lighter than the dense fabric of the creature's uniform or suit. A hand with a rounded thumb and three slender fingers with no fingernails gestured toward the camera as the alien spoke. "My world is known to you as Zeta Reticuli. It is far from your planet." Zypteron's voice resonated with an otherworldly quality, translated into human language in a voice that sounded both artificial and electronic. "Knowledge of our existence has been revealed to some among your species, but it is now for a broader understanding to unfold."

Zypteron leaned further toward the camera with large, unblinking eyes. "We have chosen this network for our communication." The alien voice continued, measured, and stilted, reflecting a totally different language structure. "We extend an invitation for you to submit your inquiries should we wish to respond. We shall return in seven days from this, when the time is twelve, Universal Time. You may signal your agreement by transmitting your inquiries by this satellite channel, preceded by a sequence of five tones."

The alien Zypteron paused. "At the designated juncture, we shall manifest once more for your broadcast, wherein some answers you seek may be revealed." The alien went on to describe the conditions of the arrangement.

With that, the alien's transmission ended, and the screen went blank.

Mark paused to settle his nerves. After a few moments, he reached to stop the recording. He pressed the IFB[1] control and said to the West Coast satellite crew, "Reschedule in one hour. Acknowledge?"

"Acknowledged," came back the reply.

Mark gathered his thoughts before dialing the extension of Richard Blaine.

Richard "Richie" Blaine was the network general manager at Nexus Broadcasting. A shrewd businessman, he rose to his position, not through a background in broadcasting, but through a series of corporate maneuvers. As with many executives in broadcasting, he had little insight into what being a broadcaster was about.

"Blaine," the manager answered. "Who's this?" he asked impatiently.

"This is Mark in satellite operations. There's something here you need to see. Can you come down?"

"Is it important?" he asked.

Mark replied with deliberation in a lowered tone, "More important than you can imagine, sir."

***

As Blaine entered the room, Mark closed the door behind him and motioned him toward the control console.

"How can I explain this? We received an unusual transmission feed today, which requires your attention."

---

1. The IFB is a special intercom circuit that consists of a mix-minus program feed sent to an earpiece worn by talent via a wire, telephone, or radio receiver (audio that is being "fed back" to talent) that can be interrupted and replaced by a television producer's or director's intercom microphone.

"Explain what?" the general manager responded, his tone a mix of curiosity and mild irritation.

Mark knew he had to tread cautiously, hoping to convey the gravity of the situation without divulging too much at once.

"Mr. Blaine," Mark began, "earlier today, while setting up for a satellite feed, something unexpected happened. The only way to explain it is for you to see it for yourself. You might want to sit down for this..." He reached for the button to play the recorded video.

As the video played, the manager leaned toward the screen and arched an eyebrow. His initial irritation gave way to fascination mixed with a hint of skepticism. "Is this real?" he questioned slowly, turning to face Mark, almost accusingly. "Surely, it's one of those, ... you know, deep fakes, right?" His tone changed. "You're tying to pull one over on me, aren't you?" Blaine clearly did not know how to deal with this situation.

Mark stopped the playback. His eyes turned to lock with Blaine's bewildered gaze. "Yes, sir. This ... alien," He pointed to the screen, "claims to be from the planet Zeta Reticuli. That matches up with the information we have been getting from our news sources lately. It would seem they have decided to reveal what our own governments, the world governments, have been unwilling to tell us."

Unconvinced, his boss challenged, "Why does it sound like that? Its lips don't even move"

Mark had an explanation. "They normally communicate telepathically. I think what we heard was some kind of translation machine." He hoped Mr. Blaine wouldn't ask how he knew that. "It overrode our one-way downlink. Nobody else saw it."

The manager's suspicions turned in another direction. Blaine leaned in and asked, "Why us? Why Nexus?"

Mark took a deep breath before responding, "You saw the recording. The alien provided no explanation for the selection. We are being offered an exclusive interview with conditions: we submit questions, but the questions need to represent different parts of the world. The alien's response will come to us in a satellite feed one week from now. We could handle it like any remote news interview. The alien will respond in the satellite feed."

Blaine pondered for a moment, his fingers tapping on the control panel. "So, we have a chance at the biggest scoop in history, is that it?"

Mark nodded. "Yes, sir. Our network would have the world's attention like never before."

Mr. Blaine considered the implications before responding, "But here's what we need to do, Mark. From now until the interview takes place, this process needs to be conducted with the utmost security. We can't let any of the other networks or, much worse, social media get even a hint of it. Not one word gets out, understood?"

Mark replied, almost like a military recruit, "Understood, sir. We'll keep this under tight wraps."

Blaine continued, now fully grasping his authority, "As for the reporters who will take part in the interview, they need think we are interviewing some high-ranking government official with secret knowledge. As the other networks have done. We can't afford to raise any suspicion."

Mark nodded in agreement, assuring his grasp of the obvious. "We'll make the arrangements, sir."

"I'm putting Emily Clark in charge of this operation. You fill her in on what's going on." With that, Blaine pointed a finger at Mark, turned and darted out of the room.

Mark dialed the number for the news director's office. Emily Clark answered on the first ring. "Emily, there's something I need to show you. Can you stop by the satellite control room?"

"Sure, Mark, is something wrong?" she asked.

"It's not that there's something wrong, but you will want to see what I recorded off the satellite feed earlier."

Emily agreed and arrived almost magically in the satellite control room a few moments later. "OK, whacha got for me?" she asked.

Again, Mark motioned toward the large monitor as he played the recorded video of the alien's message. This time, he played the entire recording, including the details of the arrangement. Privately, Mark felt uneasy as the alien appeared on the screen.

"Have you shown this to Richie?" she asked.

"I did, and he put it all in your hands," Mark responded.

Emily replied with a grimace. She slapped the side of her head with her palm, glancing skyward. "Of *course* he did."

"Richie said we can't let any of the other networks or social media get wind of it."

"No kidding!" she said knowingly. "OK, this is how we work it: I'll fill in Michael and Sarah before the broadcast so they don't fall apart in shock on the air. Nobody else needs to know. We'll have to give Alex Ramirez some kind of made-up story so he doesn't come unglued and start pushing the wrong camera buttons or forget to push any button while we're live. And under no circumstances is Rachel to get any hint of what is happening."

Rachel Turner, the online director, was already deep into conspiracy theories. There was no way she could be trusted to keep a secret like this.

Emily stopped and looked up at the ceiling, and her eyes traced her path toward the door as she was leaving. "I didn't need this. I've lost enough sleep over all the political crap."

After Emily left the room, Mark glanced at the clock and turned his attention to the West Coast feed.

Emily had a lot on her shoulders. For many reasons, they decided to pre-record the interview questions. In the few remaining hours of the day, she began contacting her selection of field reporters and stringer[2] reporters, telling them to prepare one question for an undisclosed person. She told them to assume it to be a high-ranking former official with special knowledge of the government's secret alien projects. Some reporters were on the other side of the world, none too happy to be awakened about something that was not a new war or world disaster. This was one assignment she didn't feel comfortable trusting to email. Emily discussed the kind of questions that would be required and asked that they text the questions to her rather than using

---

2. A "stringer" reporter is someone who is under contract to a news service, paid by the story and not on salary.

email. They would need to await her response before recording their questions. She set a three-day deadline for the feeds to be transmitted and screened for her approval prior to the broadcast date.

Emily provided Carol Anderson with only enough information to generate the Teleprompter scripts for reporter lead-ins for the on-the-air anchors. Janna Morrison would need to set up the lower-third titles for the reporters on the Chyron,[3] but that could come later. Maya Silverstone, with her usual artistic genius, could come up with the promo graphics, of course. Each in its turn.

That night, as Mark tried to sleep, he kept having flashbacks to his personal close encounter. It had been years since that terrifying night, but the memories returned to haunt him. He tossed and turned in his bed, the room lit by the soft glow of his alarm clock marking the hours. Images from the past flooded his mind. He saw the blinding light. He revisited the sensation of weightlessness and the feeling of being pulled upward against his will. Mark felt his heart beating fast as he remembered being in a strange corridor with gray creatures with big eyes and long limbs looking at him with intensity. The memories were so vivid, so visceral, that he could almost smell the sterile, metallic scent of the alien craft. He had told no one of his experience and was certain he never could.

Desperate to shake off the memories, Mark reached for the water bottle on his nightstand. He took several deep breaths, trying to steady his hand. This was different, he told himself. The alien was there to communicate. He was in no personal danger. This time.

The fear lingered. Mark knew he had to overcome his terror for the sake of the network, his job, and the historic event that was about to take place. He closed his eyes and focused on the rhythmic sound of his own breathing, determined to push the past

---

3. A Chyron is a text-based graphic overlay displayed at the bottom of a television screen or film frame, as closed captioning or the crawl of a newscast, named for the Chyron corporation, much as the word Xerox has come to mean any copy machine.

to the recesses of his mind and face the extraordinary encounter that awaited him and the world. Still, he was sure the nightmares would return.

***

Back at the network the next day, a feeling of urgency affected the entire staff, even those who had no clue what was going on behind the scenes. Maya Silverstone, the graphics artist, stopped Mark in the hall to ask him what was happening. Her obsession with detail went beyond fonts and formatting. As any true artist, she was sensitive to the world around her and had sensed the urgency in the building. Mark dismissed her fears by telling her, "We've got a big story in the works. You'll be filled in on it soon enough," as he smiled and pressed past her to the satellite feed center and locked the door behind him.

Later that day, Mark received an internal email from Emily listing the first of the scheduled feeds from the overseas field reporters. She must have worked all night reviewing and approving the questions. The reporters' satellite feeds continued for the rest of the week.

By the end of the week, everything was ready. As the time ticked away toward the special event, Mark had a sudden fear that the alien would not be there, that it had been a hoax after all. He steadied his nerves as the alien appeared on the large satellite monitor screen, awaiting the start of the broadcast. Mark accessed the satellite talk-back channel, hoping the alien could hear him, as he questioned, "Soundcheck?".

Zypteron responded: "Soundcheck." Mark decided the alien must have seen the movie "Network."

Pressing the call button again, Mark replied, "Soundcheck, confirmed. Ready."

Mark did not punch the switcher to send the satellite feed to Alex Ramirez in the network control room just yet. His video monitor for the "program" feed from the control room blinked on with a wide shot of the news anchors seated at the news desk. The studio lights dimmed and brightened as lighting director Robert Carter programmed the automatic controls. The Chyron displayed various titles. Carol had come through with her usual genius, with a SIG slide that said what it needed to without giving away the secret that was to be revealed. As the program monitor switched back to the wide shot of the studio, the makeup artist was putting touches of powder on news anchor Sarah Sommers to dull any light reflections.

As she faced the camera, Sarah's personality switched on like one of the studio lights. She was at once both magnetic and relatable as she twirled a pencil like a miniature baton.

Beside her, Michael Malone, the other news anchor, shuffled through papers on his desk, periodically looking up at the floor director, who was nervously pacing between the studio cameras and talking into his headset.

A large transparent plastic Nexus Broadcasting Network logo spread across the front of the news desk. Behind the host anchors was a graphic of a world map, looking more like a scene from the Matrix.

Through the glass, the control room was a flurry of activity. Lisa Reynolds operated three remote cameras, adjusting the zoom and focus for the news desk and the mystery interview guest's big screen. She set each of the remaining cameras for medium close-up shots of the news hosts.

Technical Director Alex Ramirez switched between the cameras. He reviewed the rundown sheet for the program, noting that each of the reporter videos showed a "ready" mode on his computer screen. His preview monitors displayed each of the studio cameras and the pre-roll of the first of the reporter videos. Everything except the satellite feed.

Out of sight of the studio floor, Sarah Anderson focused on the Teleprompter control. Next to her, Rachel, the Online Director, was busy setting up the social media feeds. People were speculating about what might be revealed in the broadcast, and social media was on fire. Would it be another revelation by Rick Doty, Stanton

Friedman, or even Bob Lazar, or would it be some mysterious anonymous CIA agent? The conspiracy theorists were already hotly battling the skeptics. Some networks said a large cigar-shaped spaceship was hovering over Atlanta, but the U.S. Space Surveillance Network had not confirmed it. The main satellite uplink was in Atlanta. Luckily, speculation among the other networks had not yet connected that event to the upcoming broadcast.

It was early for almost everyone on the crew. The broadcast, set for noon Universal Time or GMT, was only eight o'clock at the New York network headquarters. They cut the last hour of the morning show for the special event. Across the world, the clock moved toward 14 hours in Germany and 5 in the afternoon in South Africa.

In the main studio, producer David Mitchel shouted on the intercom, "Two minutes to live!"

Mitchel had learned the secret only moments before. The thought had crossed his mind that this momentous televised event could make Orwell's *We suggest you restructureWar of the Worlds* look like a rehearsal for the Macy's Day Parade.

In the communication headsets, TD (Technical Director), Alex Ramirez, called for the opening camera shots. He clicked the intercom to the satellite control center: "Ready on remote." For the first time, Mark let the crew see the alien. All eyes stared in amazement at the program monitor. A second passed, then five. The crew then accepted the reality of the situation and got back to their responsibilities. After all, they were professionals who had witnessed live reports from war zones.

The floor director, holding a clipboard with the Run Sheet in one hand and raising a finger on the other, called out the countdown to airtime. "Five … four… three … two….. " (The "one" was silent.) At zero, his finger dropped, pointing to anchor Michael Malone.

"Good day," Malone began, focused intently on the Teleprompter text projected onto the glass in front of the camera lens. "To say that this is a moment in history is to minimize the impact this event will have on the world. To provide a background for today's special interview, our special guest, who you are about to meet, appeared unexpectedly on our satellite feed. At first, we were not sure if what we were seeing was real. In this day, anything is possible." Malone stiffened as he leaned forward. "But I can assure you, our guest is real."

The director switched to camera three and Sommers: "Our reporters today represent a cross-section of world cultures. We have selected a sampling of our NBN reporters from around the world, from Canada to Mexico, from Germany to South Africa, to India, as well as here in the United States. Our reporters have not seen or met our special guest, but you will now." The camera switched to the studio-wide shot to show the giant screen. Zypteron nodded to the unseen audience.

The floor director raised his arm and motioned for Malone to face the left camera for a close-up as he continued. "We begin in Berlin, Germany, with NBN reporter Klaus Müller."

The video from Klaus Müller began: "I would like to ask a question that has been on the minds of many in our country and, perhaps, around the world. It has been long rumored that our earlier German government once sought to establish an Antarctic base with the goal of contacting extraterrestrial beings. Can you tell us whether those rumors are true?"

Ramirez switched to the satellite feed as Zypteron spoke: "The base you refer to was known as Base 211 or New Swabia. We can confirm that there was a base established. We became aware of the intentions of that government and did not involve ourselves in the activities. There were experiments conducted at that facility, but those experiments failed to achieve any of the goals for world dominance."

Sarah was next tasked with introducing the reporter from Canada. "Now, here is Morgan Riley in Montreal."

"Hello," the reporter began, "Can you provide any insight into the many reports of human abductions and whether they were, indeed, conducted by beings from beyond our world?"

In his office, in satellite control, Mark Foster squirmed in his chair.

Zypteron responded: "The reports of abductions hold elements of truth, but they are not uniform in their accuracy. Incidents have been conducted by beings from different places beyond your world. These activities are driven by a quest to understand life on your planet. At times, it has been necessary for us to secure what you identify as DNA for our research. However, we are aware that many of these reports lack basis in true events."

Michael Malone made the next introduction. "I'm sure this next question will generate a great deal of controversy. We considered whether to present this question to our guest. However, in view of the source of the question, we will include this question from Antonio Ricci, our reporter at the Vatican.

"In the Christian Tradition," Ricci began, "we have long revered the Star of Bethlehem as the guiding light that led three wise men to the birthplace of our Lord Jesus Christ. However, in the face of scientific study, it is difficult to explain how a distant star could serve as a moving guide. Some have asserted that the light could have been something else. I would dare to pose this question: could it be that the Star of Bethlehem was not a celestial event but rather an alien craft that guided the wise men on their journey to that holy place?"

The studio crew froze in their places as they anticipated what might come next. Viewing the broadcast from his office, Richard Blaine couldn't help but think, "*THAT* will be in ALL the papers!"

Zypteron also paused, contemplating the effect of a reply. "We can acknowledge that beings from beyond your world have taken part in certain historic events, including those involving religious figures of various belief structures." The picture remained on the alien until it was clear there would be no more to the reply.

Sarah Sommers waited to collect herself as she took in a deep breath and looked to the Teleprompter for her next introduction. "Amina Kamara provides us with the next question for our guest, from Niger, in West Africa."

"Legend in our country has led to speculation that the Dogon people of our continent had direct contact with extraterrestrial beings, who imparted knowledge of a star invisible to the human eye. Can you provide any insight into the basis of this legend?"

"Throughout the history of your planet, many species of beings have made contact with humans. These interactions have taken many forms through time, involving shared knowledge and experiences. This legend you indicate is one such example."

The camera switched to Michael Malone: "Maria Fernandez has the next question for our guest. Maria wants to know about the Mayan Pyramids and other structures in Central and South America. Here is Maria's question."

"The world has long marveled at the architectural wonders of our ancient civilizations. Many have speculated about extraterrestrial involvement in the construction of these amazing constructs. The intricate Pumapunku structures in Bolivia or the inspiration of the Nazca lines in Peru. Perhaps you might reveal something about these speculations."

"The Mayan Pyramids, Pumapunku, and the Nazca Lines are indeed remarkable human achievements, but they also bear traces of cosmic influence. Pumapunku's precision stonework was meant to harness the planet's natural energies. As for the Nazca Lines, they were a response to a brief exposure of the native peoples to our contact, much as the Amazon natives once created a straw effigy after an aircraft flew over their village."

Sarah Sommers delivered the lead-in for the next reporter's question: "We now move to India and our reporter there, Rakesh Kapoor."

The reporter began, "Throughout our history in India, there has been speculation regarding the construction of the ancient temples at Khajuraho, known for the intricate carvings and celestial depictions. Some have proposed that these temples might have been influenced or guided by extraterrestrial beings, possibly because of their remarkable architectural precision and astronomical alignments. Could you kindly share your insights on the origins of these magnificent structures and whether there might be any connection to beings from beyond our world?"

The alien seemed to have expected the question: "It would be correct to say there was involvement in these temples of beings not native to your planet. They shared knowledge of celestial alignments and construction techniques."

Zypteron continued: "Khajuraho temples represent a bridge between your planet and the cosmos, a testament to cooperation between your species and others beyond the stars. They stand as a legacy of cosmic collaboration."

Malone introduced the final reporter: "Our last question comes to us from Las Vegas, Nevada, and Rebecca Mitchel."

She had likely assumed her question was for a high-ranking official in the intelligence community. "Reports of alien involvement in nuclear incidents have been circulating," she began. "I would include the example of Malmstrom Air Force Base, where a... an aircraft... was observed coincidentally with the disabling of nuclear missiles. Prior to that, there are accounts of alien presence during the testing of the first atomic bomb in New Mexico." Rebecca paused; her expression turned earnest as she continued. "Can you provide insight into those events? Have beings from beyond our world been present during these events? "

The alien pulled back and stiffened as it answered: "It is true that cultures in the universe have become concerned over certain activities on your planet. The destructive and disruptive potential of nuclear devices poses a threat not only to your species but to the balance of life in the universe. At certain times, restraint has been deemed necessary to safeguard the future of the galaxy and to protect the intricate tapestry of life that exists. You may expect these efforts to continue."

As the alien interview came to a close, the camera view moved to a two-shot of the hosts. The image of the alien dissolved away and was replaced by a graphic featuring the moon and stars on the large screen. The news anchors, Michael Malone, and Sarah Sommers, exchanged solemn glances. The weight of the moment hung in the air, and it was time for them to deliver their closing statements to the world.

In a dramatic close-up camera shot, Michael Malone turned to face the camera. His steady expression conveyed his thoughtfulness as he summarized the historic event.

"We have touched the fringes of a reality long feared, a reality that challenges our understanding of the universe and our place in it."

Sarah Sommers continued the message, her voice measured and precise. "The impact of this encounter will undoubtedly spark discussions, debates, and soul-searching across the globe. For some, it may shatter preconceived notions of the cosmos, while for others, it may affirm long-held beliefs."

Michael nodded; his gaze was unwavering as both anchor hosts faced the center camera. "There will be controversy, there will be speculation, there will be accusations, but the truth is often hard to accept and harder still to understand."

Sarah echoed his sentiments, her eyes reflecting a mix of hope and trepidation. "As we move forward, let us remember that knowledge, even when it challenges us, has the power to unite humanity in our shared quest for understanding."

Michael concluded with a note of unity. "We are witnesses to a moment in history, a moment that calls upon us to come together as a species, to embrace the unknown, and to strive for a future where we explore not only the cosmos but the depths of our own potential."

The screen transitioned to a Nexus Broadcasting Network logo over a spinning Earth and a background of stars. And that was how it ended. The closing statements left the world to contemplate the profound implications of the alien encounter, a moment that would resonate for generations.

Or, at least until the next network program.

If Ghosts Could Talk

"What's that thing do?" Jack looked over Alex's shoulder at a device plugged into a USB port on his laptop computer. Alex has always been the one for techy things, while Jack is more into adventure.

"It's a radio. It's a radio controlled by a program on my computer. It's called a Software Digital Radio. It's really an updated version of the old scanner radios."

The SDR, as it is called, looks like a USB flash drive on one end and an antenna "F" connection on the other. It is largely used by the military and amateur radio enthusiasts. The simplest models have a tuning range from 500 kHz to 18 GHz and can be found for less than $50 on Amazon.

Jack looks puzzled. "What's wrong with a regular radio?"

"A digital radio lets me listen to any frequency," Alex explained. "I can tune in all kinds of signals. FM, AM, the military, police, and aircraft have different frequencies. I want to see what I can find."

Jack couldn't see anything interesting about that. "So, what are you looking for, then?"

"Maybe I can find something hidden, like maybe the FBI, or drug smugglers, or NASA's private channel," and Alex smiled, " or even space aliens. Who knows?"

Alex connected the antenna to the digital radio device plugged into the laptop. The antenna looked something like old TV "rabbit ears, with a cable coming out from the bottom. He ran the program on the laptop computer, and the screen displayed the frequencies from left to right with tiny vertical spikes, looking like the side view of lawn grass. The display is sometimes described as a waterfall. The speakers hissed and crackled with static.

Jack squinted at the screen, his eyes fixed on a sharp spike on the left side of the display. "So, what's that?" he asked, pointing to the screen.

Alex frowned. "That's weird. That's a very low frequency. I'm not sure what it is. He turned up the speakers and switched between FM to sideband to some of the digital options. Finally, when he selected Amplitude Modulation or AM mode, they heard a low hum, more like a moan.

"Well, what is it? Can you figure it out?" Jack asked impatiently.

Alex tried moving a few of the filters and settings on the screen. "Let's see... it's definitely not a regular station way down on that frequency. Lower frequencies can go a long way, so there's no telling where it's coming from."

"What is it, then?" Jack asked, leaning over Alex's shoulder.

Alex shrugged. "It could be almost anything." He was about to continue with his explanation when the signal spike disappeared, and that section of the screen display went almost flat, except for background noise.

Jack frowned. "What do we do now? Wait for it to show up again?"

Alex nodded. "Yeah, I'll keep checking and see if I can. Maybe we can even track it down. "

Jack looked skeptical. "But what if it's something really creepy, like a secret government experiment or something? Hey! It might be time for a new adventure!"

Alex and Jack liked to go on adventures with their other college friends, Maya, Liam, and Emma. The group formed in a science class at the local college when they discovered they all shared a special kind of curiosity.

Although Alex assumed the role of the tech guru in the group, Jack was more of a thrill seeker. He considered himself an adventurer, always looking for exciting things to do. Sometimes Jack found Alex dull, but Alex managed to capture his attention. That's likely why he often came to visit to see what Alex had going on.

Emma might have been the leader of the group or the organizer, depending on your point of view. She could also be described as resourceful. She seemed to have the answer to most any problem the group encountered, and they had encountered quite a few challenges.

Maya, unlike the others, possessed a profound connection to the energies of the universe. Her mind remained receptive to all possibilities, be they extraordinary or ordinary. She unabashedly embraced her belief in the paranormal.

In stark contrast to Maya, Liam identified as a realist—a description that could easily be replaced by the word *skeptic*. He prided himself on his unyielding logic, never hesitating to characterize himself as logical. From his perspective, there's always a rational explanation awaiting discovery if one seeks it.

Early the next day, Alex texted Jack, "It's back! What do you say we find out where it's coming from?"

The antenna comprised two telescoping rods. A small tripod connected to the base where the wire came out. He hooked it to the USB device which plugged into the laptop computer. While bulky, it remained manageable. Shaping the antenna into a "V" focused the sensitivity. Alex methodically rotated the antenna, adjusting the inside of the "V" to face various directions until the mystery signal appeared the strongest.

Alex knew it would be hard to juggle the laptop with the antenna attached to the digital radio dongle. That's why he sent a text message to Jack asking for help.

When Jack arrived, Alex passed him the laptop and held the antenna as they made their way outside. Once there, Alex began a circular path, holding on to the antenna while Jack followed with the laptop. Avoiding stumbles while monitoring the display proved to be a challenge. After repeating the pattern several times, Alex decided the signal was strongest toward the northwest.

Time for reinforcements. Alex called Emma and filled her in on what he and Jack had been doing. He had to explain to Emma what a digital radio was, but she caught on.

"What do you need me to do?" she asked.

"You could drive us around in your convertible while Jack and I try to figure out where this mystery signal is coming from," Jack explained.

Fully in on the adventure, Emma exclaimed, "I'll call Maya and Liam to see if they're up to joining in." Since it was Saturday, assembling the group for a new adventure was no problem. As a group, they resembled a live-action Scooby-Doo team, albeit without the talking dog or the van.

When Emma and the others arrived at Alex's house, Maya and Liam were in the front seat while Alex and Jack climbed in the back. As they drove around, Alex called out directions... "Find a way to go left... no, the other way!"

In the hills outside of Whispering Pines, the signal appeared to be coming from an old cemetery. On the top of a hill behind the cemetery stood a massive, ancient house, or maybe it was an old mansion. The colonial structure resembled something out of a horror movie. Even from a distance, they could make out intricate carvings on the doors. The siding on the old wooden structure, weathered and worn, was punctuated by deep grooves and knots. Glints of sunlight reflected from the diamond-shaped glass panels in the tall, narrow windows. The roof had a steep slope, with metal shingles in different stages of rust. Above the roofline, the chimney tilted precariously to one side. Sections of the wide front porch sagged, revealing the surrender of the wooden structure to gravity. The old house exuded a blend of grandeur and decay.

Maya looked up at the old building. "Well, if it isn't haunted, it certainly has the potential to be," she said with some amount of satisfaction.

By now, Alex had been watching the mystery radio signal get stronger, but as the car slowed to a stop, it faded away. Alex and the

others waited for something to happen, but
the computer display remained quiet.

Maya's frown showed disappointment. "Maybe it saw us!"

"How do we know this is where the signal is coming from?" asked Liam.

Alex didn't have an answer. "We don't, really, but it looked like it came from that direction," he said, pointing toward the old mansion up the hill. "But I guess we'll have to try again another time."

"That house looks like something out of the Adams Family," Jack said.

"Or The Munsters, more likely," Liam suggested.

Emma had her phone out, checking Google Maps. "I'm not sure how to get up there," she admitted.

At this point, Jack was showing his disappointment. The adventure he had anticipated would not materialize. At least not that day.

So, disappointed, the group headed back to Alex's house, stopping along the way at their favorite ice cream shop, of course.

***

Early Sunday morning, Alex once again had the digital radio to check for the mysterious signal. Sure enough, there it was again. He sent a group text to the others in their group: "It's back. Anybody up to giving it another try?" After a few minutes, everybody texted back. Yes, they were ready to go.

That previous evening, Emma devised a way to get to the old mansion. On reaching the cemetery, she turned on an old dirt road hidden by branches and debris. Alex and Jack got out to clear the way. The roadway had seen no traffic for quite a long time. Liam commented how it struck him as odd not to see any "no trespassing" signs, much less a "for sale" sign. As they reached the old house, they found the front door sagging open, the hinges having long since tired of holding onto the frame.

Once inside, Alex set up the computer on the folding table. As the group watched, he checked the display. This time, the signal was back, and it was even stronger than before. But as he guided the antenna around in a pattern, the signal display remained the same. "I think it's here.... somewhere," Alex announced to the group.

"Well, I guess we didn't scare it off this time," said Maya. "This place is still really creepy, though."

Liam suggested they explore the house to see what they could find.

As Liam, Maya, and Jack went to explore, Emma stayed behind, and Alex tried the settings to see if he could decode the signal. He switched through all the settings. When he finally went back to the AM setting, the speaker barked with a strange rumbling sound. The noise brought the others back from their tour of the old mansion.

"What's it saying?" Jack asked as he peered at the computer display.

Alex, still adjusting, "It's not *SAYING* anything," he grumbled, glancing over his shoulder at the others.

Emma put her hands on her hips and shook her head. "There's nothing here. There's certainly no electricity for anything to run on."

Maya was feeling a little frightened. "What if ghosts can talk?" She jumped as the sound of the laptop speaker changed, almost in response, as it emitted a series of bursts of staccato pulses.

"That's no kind of ghost I ever heard of," Liam said. "Sounds more like some kind of data."

"We're not on a digital setting. It's still on AM," Alex answered. He tried the other settings again, but with no success. "Certainly not digital," he concluded. As the noise continued, Alex clicked on the recording function so the software could capture what they were hearing.

"Maybe it's a robot," Emma suggested.

"What would a robot be doing in a house like this?" Maya asked.

Jack had a thought. "Maybe there's a basement."

Jack and Emma left the others to look. A short time later, they came back to report finding a stairway to the darkness below. They decided not to venture into its depths.

Alex sighed. "Well, that's it for today. The signal's gone again."

Now what?" Liam asked as he came down the stairs. Like the others, he was disappointed.

Alex grimaced and shook his head. "I've been watching it for a while when you guys went looking around. It's definitely gone quiet."

"Are you sure?" Emma asked.

"While it was there, I made a recording," he said. "I think I know who might be able to help us. There's somebody I want to play it for."

***

Alex's morning classes lasted until noon that Monday. After lunch, he went to find Dr. Emily Jameson in the science department. Luckily, she was in her office. He knocked on the door. She put aside the papers she was grading and invited him in.

Dr. Jameson, in her early 40s, had short blond hair and glasses. Previously a researcher in electromagnetic radiation and its effects on the human body for a government agency, she grew weary of bureaucracy and politics. Leaving that world behind, she pursued her passion for teaching and became a physics professor at the College of Arts and Sciences. Enjoying the more informal setting, she found fulfillment in interacting with students and sharing her knowledge with them.

"Do I know you?" she asked. "Are you one of my students this year?"

"I was in one of your classes last year," he said. "I wonder if you could help me solve a mystery?" Alex pulled the digital radio dongle out of his pocket and laid it on the desk. "I've been experimenting with this."

"What is it?" Dr. Jameson asked.

"It's an SDR: a software digital radio. I plug it into my laptop, and I can listen to almost any frequency and transmission type," Alex explained.

"OK, I know about those. I've never seen one. So how can I help you?" the professor asked.

"I found this on a very low frequency." Alex had copied the recording to his phone, and he played the sound from the computer program. "What do you think it is?"

The professor was silent for a moment. Her head turned at an angle toward Alex while she thought. "You probably know VLF or Very Low Frequencies could come from anything from lightning to geomagnetic activity. Where did you hear it?"

Alex explained how they ended up at the old cemetery a few blocks from his house. He admitted the group had gone looking for clues in the old house since they found it open and with no "keep out" signs on the property.

"What else is around there?" Dr. Jameson asked.

Alex couldn't recall seeing anything but the old cemetery.

"I think we can rule out any geomagnetic activity," she said. "I don't remember any thunderstorms so far this month. That really doesn't sound like lightning static, anyway. There might be some power grid wires nearby. It could even come from underground pipes. The hospital is on the other side of town, so that would probably rule out EEG machines or magnetometers."

Surprised, Alex remarked, "I didn't realize there's so much stuff on low frequencies."

"You've certainly got my curiosity up," said the instructor. "I might want to check it out with you. How about this weekend?"

Alex never expected the professor to take an interest in the mystery. They agreed to meet at Alex's house early on Saturday morning. Alex thanked the professor. He couldn't wait to tell the others, so he typed out a group text as he walked through the hallways to his last class of the day. They were all set for the weekend!

***

Not everyone could fit in Emma's car Saturday morning, so Dr. Jameson followed in her own car, so Alex and Jack rode with her. They loaded the laptop gear and a small folding table in the back of the professor's SUV.

Upon reaching the old house, Alex set up the laptop on the folding table in the main entry. The rest of the group checked to be sure no one else ...or no-*thing* else was in the house while the professor circled around to the back of the property. On her return, Alex was engrossed in the screen, moving the antenna.

"I think I know where your mystery signal is coming from," she said to Alex. "You said it seems to come and go, like the wind. Am I right? Did you notice the windmills in the field behind the house?"

Alex shook his head no. The windmills had escaped his attention.

"I'm guessing that there is some kind of defect in one of the wind turbines. When the wind is exactly right, it vibrates. I can hear it rattle. It's possible for wind turbines to generate low-frequency waves."

She went on, "Those waves can travel through the ground, creating a sympathetic resonance. That's what you see on your digital radio. It's unusual but not impossible. If you move your radio to the back porch, you can watch for your radio signal as the windmills turn."

Maya came down the stairs from exploring the second floor and heard the last part of the conversation. She helped Alex carry the computer and the setup on the back porch. Sure enough, the signal on the screen went away when the windmill stopped turning.

Professor Jameson explained, "The key to this mystery is understanding electromagnetic resonance. We know this part of the state has a history of iron mines. It is possible that a network of tunnels is deep underground, under this old house. Over time, it's possible that over time, some of the exposed iron has corroded and formed peculiar shapes, acting as a natural tuned cavity."

Alex broke in, "You're saying the tunnels could be resonating with the radio waves from the windmills?"

"Exactly," Dr. Jameson confirmed. The windmills have electric components that generate magnetic fields. When the wind blows, it creates vibrations. The vibrations, in turn, resonate with corroded iron deposits in underground tunnels, magnifying electronic waves."

Jack was impressed. "So, it's like a natural radio transmitter?"

"That's right. The signal on your little receiver comes from a unique electromagnetic resonance phenomenon. No paranormal forces, only science."

Alex nodded in understanding.

"I have an idea that it won't be long before the windmill maintenance people repair the problem, and your radio signal will go away," the professor added.

"I was really hoping for ghosts," Maya confessed.

Jack spoke up, "I guess it's like the old song! The answer was *blowing in the wind* all along!"

Dr. Jameson smiled. "No, I was just kidding, it was really ghosts."

As they all headed back to the cars to leave the old house, Emma suggested, "How about some ice cream?"

Date Night

"What shall we do?" he asked. "We can go anywhere we want."

Henry and Evelyn sat on the front porch of their Florida beach-front home.

Now in her 80s, Evelyn, or "Eve" Thompson, still carried an air of elegance. Her soft, silver hair was always neatly coiffed. She dipped her head, and her hazel eyes gazed at her husband over the rim of her sunglasses.

"What would *you* like to do?" she asked. "It's been so long since you've taken me on a date."

Hank returned her gaze with his usual charming smile; his once-thick dark hair, now reduced to a few tufts of silver, glinting in the late afternoon sunlight.

"We always do everything together," Hank argued.

"That's not the same as a date," Eve protested.

"I suppose you're right," he replied. "You usually are." His smile broadened as he cocked his head to one side. "But this time it should be something special."

Eve brushed her hair away from her face. She seemed to view a scene in the distance, or perhaps in the past. "What did you have in mind?"

"I think it should be something we both enjoy." Hank's forehead formed a crease above his eyes as he searched his mind for an idea.

"Remember that time we went on Bob and Helen's sailboat?" Eve punctuated her statement with a soft chuckle. "You wore a captain's hat."

"I'd like to *forget* that if you don't mind. I got sick halfway across the bay. And there weren't any waves!" Hank shook his head and looked to the porch ceiling and back toward his wife of sixty years. "No, nothing involving small boats is on my list." After a moment, he added sadly, "Bob and Helen are gone now, anyway."

"What will they say about us?" she pondered.

"I'm sure they'll say nice things, and some of them might be true!"

A small bird came to a landing on the porch railing with a chirp, ignoring the couple as if they weren't there before it turned and flew off to a branch on a nearby bush.

"I bet you don't remember our first date."

"Bet I do. We were just out of high school. All I had was a bicycle, but somehow, you talked your father into letting me drive his car. We went to get..."

"We went to get ice cream," Eve finished Hank's sentence for him. "And as we sat in the car and talked, it felt as if my dad was watching."

"In a way, he was."

They both chuckled at the thought.

"Did you go on many dates before you met me?" Eve asked.

Hank's face took on a sheepish smile. "No, could you guess? I wasn't any good at dating. I had to be back home by 10 and I spent most of my allowance on things like a transistor radio. The girls I knew, well, they didn't find me interesting. I don't blame them. I was never comfortable with girls my age. That was until I met you."

"Do you remember the first thing we agreed on?"

Hank laughed. "Yeah, we agreed we would never get married! And see how that turned out, now sixty years later."

"And you never proposed, either. You said, 'When do you think we should get married?'".

"But you didn't object."

"No, of course not." Eve cocked her head to one side with a wink.

He reached over and laid his hand on hers as they watched a flock of seabirds flying in formation high in the sky. Eve turned to Hank and smiled. Then she slipped her hand free and reached over to straighten his hair a bit.

"If we had children, they would be reaching their own retirement now."

Hank chuckled softly. "Can you imagine? By now there might have been grandchildren coming to visit us here."

"Things would certainly have been different. We might not have been as free to travel; London, Paris, summers camping the mountains ..."

"I suppose, but a part of me wonders what it might have been like to have shared those adventures with children, to watch their children grow, and be a part of their lives."

Hank leaned back in his chair, a smile spreading across his face as he imagined what could have been.

Finally, he said, "We still haven't decided what to do."

"We could go for ice cream."

"That doesn't sound very exciting."

"It *was* back then when we were first dating." She smiled.

For a moment, they were both lost in thought.

At long last, Hank suggested, "Let's go sit on the beach and watch the ocean.".

Eve nodded in agreement. They got up and walked together down the porch steps, along the trail through the sea grasses, toward the sound of the waves. As they walked, Hank reached out and took Eve's hand. They shared a warm glance as they followed the sandy pathway through the tall grasses.

The sand had buried two old Adirondack chairs a few inches deep, providing anchorage against the wind and waves. In the sky above, the sun painted the clouds with a red glow.

Hank gestured toward one chair, bowing low, imitating the gesture of a *maitre d*. Eve curtsied, brushed off a bit of sand and took her place in the chair. Hank smiled and took his place in the other.

Between them and the waves, sand crane scurried across the wet sand, chasing after the retreating surf. The evening breeze carried the salty mist from the water lapping against the shoreline.

Eve closed her eyes and tilted her head upward. "I could enjoy sitting here together forever."

Hank matched her motion and closed his eyes. "Then that's exactly what we'll do."

The night fell, the sun faded, and so, too, did the couple holding hands on the beach.

As ghosts are wont to do.

Please Review!

If you enjoyed this book, please take a few moments to write a nice review where you purchased it and recommend it to your friends and social media followers! You can also find a review form on my website at TimTro ttWrites.com. If you find things that need the author's attention, please share in the contact form.

About the Author

Isaac Asimov, or Aldous Huxley and perhaps Philip K. Dick, or Ray Bradbury inspired Tim Trott's writing style. Of course! Tim grew up reading Asimov and Huxley, along with Franklin .W. Dixon (*Hardy Boys*). Those authors were bound to have an influence.

His fiction writing combines elements of psychological thriller, science, and speculative fiction. The narrative style is engaging, with a focus on character experiences and internal conflicts, which draws the reader into the protagonist's psychological journey. If you look closely, you may find an underlying narrative.

He is a writer who is passionate about investigation and shedding light on important issues. Tim Trott's writing, whether fiction or non-fiction, demonstrates a commitment to research and an adeptness in communicating complex topics with clarity, skills honed during his early career in broadcasting.

A lifelong student and observer of current events and issues, Tim brings a wealth of perspective and insight into his work. Despite not being a well-known author, his writing holds value because of the information he provides and the quality of his communication. His writing is a testament to a lifetime spent in diverse occupations, each contributing to a tapestry of perspectives on the complex issues shaping our world.

Research informs Tim Trott's writing. His exploration of this multifaceted topic goes beyond the headlines, delving into the nuances that often escape casual observation. Drawing on the skills cultivated throughout his career, Tim navigates the subject's complexities with a balanced and informed perspective.

Beyond the mere presentation of facts, Tim's writing reflects a commitment to fostering understanding and informed dialogue. His ability to distill intricate information into accessible narratives makes his work informative and engaging for readers from all walks of life.

In his post-retirement years, Tim Trott has found a renewed purpose in contributing to the discourse surrounding critical societal issues. Through his writing, he continues to share his wealth of knowledge, providing readers with the tools they need to form well-informed opinions on the pressing matters of our time.

Member: Florida Writers Association (FWA) and Florida Authors and Publishers Association (FAPA).

Tim Trott invites you to visit his website at TimTrottWrites.com.

Please consider these other books by the author:

Science Fiction/Paranormal:

- *What If... (Vol 1),*

- *What If... (Vol 2),*

- *The Brown Bean Coffee Shoppe (Book one)*

Biography:

- *Out of the Blue: The Life and Legend of Kirby "Sky King" Grant,*

- *First Through the Fire (the story of Talbert Gray)*

Education:

- *Understanding WordPress 6.x for Beginners,*
- *FAA UAG 107 Remote Pilot Study Guide,*
- *Drone Operations*

Security:

- *Guarding Against Online Identity Theft*
- *Proteccion de Identidad*

Politics/History:

- *T is for Treason, Broken Border,*
- *Party of NO,*
- *Trumped*

Misc/LCB:

- *LOTTO TRAKR*